Edinburgh Shorts

By

Cooperative of Creative Writers

To contact any of the authors or the editorial and production team please email:
edinburghshorts@holyroodbooks.co.uk

ISBN: 9781849142946

Foreward

Joyce Holmes

There can be few cities in the world that offer more scope to the writer than does Edinburgh. Here we see her in many moods and from different perspectives, as she was in the past and as she is today. It can be too easy to take her for granted, registering only the familiar face we encounter every day but to see her through the eyes of someone who has really *looked* can be a rewarding experience.

That, in a way, is what writers are for: Sometimes we need someone to do the *looking* for us: to take the time to dream and to imagine in a way that is not easy in the turmoil of everyday life. And what a privilege it is to see the world through these thoughtful eyes and to have our own eyes opened to what would otherwise go unnoticed.

The Writers' Cooperative has given us an in depth appreciation of Edinburgh from a diversity of viewpoints, forming a patchwork from which emerges a deeper, more intense appreciation of Scotland's magnificent capital.

Joyce Holmes is the best selling crime author of "Payment Deferred" and the Fizz & Buchanan series.

Contents

The cover image is provided by Gerry Gapinski

Website : www.gerrygapinski.com

Writer's Cooperative – Journeys

Andy Nairn, Sarah Guppy and Janette Crawford

The drive through the town has been uneventful, almost relaxed. Rising from Leith I drive along old streets with hastily cobbled together "bus and taxi" lanes in an effort to keep the snake of empty public transport running at the cost of the people trying to get somewhere in their car.

Avoiding the roads which have been cut up for tram rails I wind a serpentine path around the back streets of the city centre, surrounded by great faux Greek columns and ornate baroque architecture on one side and open grass speckled with dog poop bins on the other. At night all this is ignored, it's challenging enough to make sure I am in the correct lane, and keeping a grip on the slick, cobbles.

A short burst of speed, a throaty roar, a flash of alfa red, and I'm over the Royal Mile's cobbles and onto South Bridge, heading for Nicholson Street, home of the Festival Theatre, but more importantly, my destination.

Andy Nairn.

***

It's a dark, damp night but thankfully my bus stop is free of fresh urine. I'm grateful for small mercies, strange habits some folk have. Fag ends adorn the ground like filthy snowflakes.

I drop coinage in to the driver's box and off we trundle towards cosmopolitan Nicholson Street. Casting curious eyes over fellow passengers, I spy a hoody listening to music, people tapping texts in to mobiles and elderly folk poised for their escape at the front. Although we're all on the bus I wonder what individual life journeys are represented here. All on the bus, but are we equally enduring the recession? Are we heck!

At the Writers Co-operative though there is semblance of equality and a rich variety of characters and writing styles too. Once off the bus I walk towards Spoon; another stimulating caffeine soaked evening awaits.

Sarah Guppy.

***

There is a long table by the window overlooking Nicholson Street. Three candles are spaced equally along its length and paper menus are laid out fan-style at its centre. There are a variety of cups filled with coffee, some topped with light froth others left a strong black. There is a floral teapot with the string of a tea-bag tied around its handle; the tea is Earl Grey, light and fragrant. The tea-pot, cups and saucers are 1950s-style, quirky yet pleasing just like the interior of the Spoon café. More people arrive; a jug of water is brought to the table, and then two shapely glasses of wine, one white, one red.

Everyone settles down, new members are welcomed and introduced. Sheets of paper are handed out, adding to the clutter on the table. 'What should we read first?' someone asks. The subjects and styles are as varied as the drinks, and as colourful as the décor.

A late-comer arrives, apologises. 'I see you have lots of paper in front of you.' he says, 'Are you the Writers' Group?' 'Yes', we say, 'Please join us.

Janette Crawford.

To Be Continued...

The Snapshot from The Mound

Sandy Bennett

Getting off the train that first day I was just one more Australian backpacker, not dressed quite appropriately for September in Edinburgh, with her camera around her neck and a big grin on her face. That night I posted one of my pictures on Facebook with the comment: "Edinburgh I have such a crush on you." Taken from The Mound the black and white picture centres on North Bridge and is bookended by the Balmoral Hotel and the Medieval Old Town.

Walking through the city everything towers monumental over you; the dark weathered stone bridges, hotels, libraries, banks, shops and churches stand together in an arresting mass of antiquity, perfectly formed to awe the tourist hordes. But in my picture the sky dwarfs all below; the city is an ornately detailed miniature. In the vast tract of sky cloud dramatically up-swirls in the top right corner dragging the eye away from the tightly erect little man-made structures at the bottom of the frame; they are a sparse third of the image. A band of fluffy cumulus sits above the bridge, cotton wool perfect. The city might be in a bottle.

The miniature world is a perfect Edinburgh moment frozen in time - the archetypal dark stone contrasts with bright bursts of afternoon sunshine glinting off the bridge, scattered windows and the tower clock face of the Balmoral Hotel. You can see Calton Hill nestled behind the Balmoral, the castellated battlements of the Governor's house are just visible, but the hill's monuments are obscured by the picture's point of view. Framing the picture squarely on North Bridge also cuts out the Scott Monument, but the blackened Gothic spires rocketing upwards steal the show so thoroughly that the ode to the Scottish literary juggernaut is almost superimposed onto the vista.

Out of the city in a bottle a few steps to the left will give you Arthur's Seat, the Firth of Forth and the contentious Parliament building. A stroll around the squat columnar buildings of the Scottish National Gallery gives you Edinburgh Castle above, and down through the bars of the fence you can see the ornate Princes Street Gardens. Beyond the borders of the picture Edinburgh's sites roll out in magnificent 3D.

The angle I chose might dissolve the train lines passing beneath The Mound, and Waverley Station, Waverley

Bridge and all the people, buses and taxies passing through that hub of arrivals and departures, but once upon-a-time non of that was even imagined. Once the whole area was a flooded valley providing protection to the castle, then The Nor' Loch became a dumping ground for the Medieval town's trash, and eventually it was filled in to form pleasure gardens. The land beneath my feet when I took my picture, though I did not known it at the time, was formed quite recently in Edinburgh's time line; two hundred or so years ago, from earth excavated during the building of the Georgian New Town. So to stand on The Mound is to stand quite literally on a palimpsest holding Edinburgh's ancient layers.

I have taken plenty of snapshots since I left Australia in May 2011, zebras in Tanzania, mosques in Istanbul, London bridges, walls in Jerusalem and cityscapes in Amman. But this picture is different. When I took it I thought I might spend a day or two in the city after my Highland adventure - walk up Arthur's Seat, visit the Castle, frequent some galleries and have a pint or three with some other backpackers before trotting off to Ireland or Norway. I was passing through, notching up snapshots on my hard-drive and stamps in my passport, I did not imagine I would ever be anything more than a tourist in this town.

But life turned itself in a new direction - the sliding doors opened and I stumbled across an interesting fellow, got a pretty stamp in my passport that says I can stay for two years, and I have set about getting a life in Edinburgh. I have unpacked my backpack into a chest of drawers, bought a coffee plunger, some new sheets, and even gotten some house keys. As I slowly unravel the city I find myself residing in, my Summer travel wardrobe is being supplemented with the essential accoutrements for my first ever Northern Winter.

My school girl crush on the city still holds forth, but like most first impressions it has deepened, gotten more complex as the layers reveal themselves. Sometimes, walking through Edinburgh I am reminded of another European city - Venice: both have vista's to die for, but they can feel like spectacular Hollywood sets, as though everything is put up for the tourists - with all the views, local novelty and souvenirs nicely packaged up and on display. Venice has stripe shirted Gondoliers and Gelato, Edinburgh has kilted bagpipers and haggis. But then I take a walk to get groceries, or get on a bus to visit a friend in Leith and I discover a whole city away from Princes Street and the Royal Mile. Now that I am working at being a local, those once hidden away sights, sounds, streets and people are part of my everyday. I am unpacking the many hidden wonders and necessities of my new hometown; tracking down the charity shops, a good fish and chipper, friendly pubs, running routes and an Asian supermarket to supply my sweet chilli sauce addiction. And like any crush turned into a full blown love affair these ins and outs all affirm and expand my first spark of delight.

The big Edinburghian set pieces still entrance me. I see Edinburgh Castle from my kitchen window, and the view of Arthur's Seat, glimpsed throughout my wanderings around town is as uplifting as it was on that first afternoon, when I followed tiny glimpses of it down the Royal Mile in hopes of getting an unimpeded snap. Oh, and that view of the Bridge I posted on Facebook all those months ago? I walk past it on my way to work now.

Each time I pass by I stop and take a picture of that same view. I know it gets snapped by every visiting tourist, but there is always something different to see - in the picture and in the fragments beyond the frame. A train, a hogmanay ferris wheel, a stunning couple, a Big Issue seller chatting to his girlfriend, girls who have forgotten to put their skirts on and usually a handsomely kilted bagpiper. One morning while American women posed with my backdrop there were a group of men across the road who had stopped to look – not at one of Edinburgh's many spectacular views, but at the crane and digger at work on the Princes Street tram line. I am learning that road works are as typical as the whine of bagpipes around here. You can rarely cross the same road in the same way twice, and even the local taxi drivers get lost. The traveller in me doesn't mind that too much, but as a wannabe local I feel obliged to complain.

With so much that is new around me my transition out of travel mode has been an easy one. Travel teaches you that everyday is an adventure - the trick is to keep that alive now that my backpack is gathering dust on top of the wardrobe. My picture taking ritual helps to reminds me to always look about me with fresh eyes, because there should never be anything mundane about your everyday. I take the picture again and again to remember that - and because I like to capture the ever changing sky.

I am more convinced everyday that the dramatic emphasis on the sky in that September snapshot is as important a part of the place as layers of ancient architecture. The sky tells me if I should leave the house today and if I am venturing out whether I should wear my warm, warmer or waterproof jacket. For this little Australian the high drama of weather in Edinburgh is as challenging as the twisty, multi-named, multi-levelled streets. Thankfully bleak winds, icy rain, snow flurries and freezing days are often relieved by those bursts of stunning sunshine I captured glinting off the bridge that first day. Unfortunately tall stone buildings and narrow streets don't lend themselves to letting the sun shine down on you.

On that first day wandering the streets I saw a powerfully built shirtless man sitting on a doorstep near the library, he was soaking up the last of the days September rays. Back then he looked a little strange, but now, in February I understand his motives perfectly. If a sunbeam happens to manage the journey down through the layers of the city and onto your face you stop and drink it in. Thankfully, my earliest non-tourist walk introduced me to the grassy expanses and tree lined footpaths of The Meadows, because when there is sunshine, it shines there.

Sun or no sun every time I walk through The Meadows I feel a little thrill of belonging. If you are walking along the Royal Mile people may well peg you as a tourist, but passing through the park-lands with students and other on foot commuters you are a local. The Meadows buskers don't play bagpipes; they play the glockenspiel, because tourists don't wander here. The park was another once upon-a-time Edinburghian Loch; the South Loch used to provided the town with drinking water, but now drained and grassy, it provides locals with a place to play rugby, twirl fire sticks and manoeuvre in ultimate Frisbee.

Even though history lessons are just as available for The Meadows as on The Mound, in the park, unlike so much of Edinburgh the now is more present than the past. I love how these time shifts accost you as you wander the streets, medieval turrets greet your eye and you imagine maidens fluttering their ribbons there, the headache-making diggers on Princes Street are at work for a better tomorrow and the ghost tour touts on the Royal Mile want to tell all about the gory past. The ever present and ever shifting cogs of time make sense to me, I live in the now, but my past is alive in each step I take, just as Edinburgh's past is alive in her streets, buildings, graveyards and her earth.

The earth of The Mound has been erased and reinscribed so many times that it hums with its layers of history. The old valley at the floor of the ancient city has risen up to become a modern lookout. Standing and looking out on the same view day after day I have come to wonder what other transformative powers the place has. Are there witches bones scattered through the earth disturbed to extend the city? Crouching between the intersecting layers of new and old Edinburgh, with train lines running through her and footsteps endlessly echoing across her; it is a very liminal spot. The Mound has seen so many journeyers pass by, I wonder if it opened up a door to me in the moment my finger snapped that black and white picture? Was that the moment my old life intersected with my new? Where would I be if I was not here? Where would that alternate reality have taken me? Which face would I see on the pillow next to mine when I wake in the morning? Which city or town would I be in? Would it be warmer? Would the heater work there?

I ponder these things, but although I know where that doorway is I am not going back through it. I like this reality just fine.

Early Morning Train from Edinburgh

Sarah Guppy

The Indian couple opposite me
sat gazing in to each other's eyes
they had gone in to a mythic time.

The woman's face not unlike
those features found in old Asian paintings
depicting jungle journeys, moments of love

inspiration in the form of a peacock.
We had all caught the early train
from Edinburgh, and outside the train

Mist still lingered on the sleeping, slumbering land.
The landscape was well suited to the lovers' state:
a magical terrain lit by a violent red sun

a hidden land, seen only by themselves and
receptive to their murmurings.
A picture of tranquillity all around then

as we trundled further South, the morning
became ever more alive, the sun a healthier yellow
with each half hour gone.

Now the lovers had broken off
their trance-like state
he, returning to his *"The Subtle Art Of Flirting"*

a slim publication, guiding readers on seductive dress;
she, shoes removed, waggling her purple toe-nailed feet.
Peace prevailed with the world at that moment

Both inside the train and out,
the lovers' state, though invisible to the naked eye
hanging as gently in the air

as the mist had hung
upon the gorse
the train being the only thing that moved.

Learning Lessons

Janette Crawford.

Duncan paused for a moment; The Mound was a steep and arduous climb and he needed to catch his breath. Resting against the railings he unfolded the glossy leaflet advertising a Tenement Museum - *"Go back in time and see how people lived in the Old Town of Edinburgh."* His initial feeling of shock when he saw the picture of the building had given way to one of disbelief, doubt, and then curiosity. He pocketed the leaflet again. He would never forgive himself if he didn't investigate.

He waited in a short queue, paid the entrance fee and once inside followed the Visitor Guide through the various rooms. He listened with interest as she talked about the people who had once lived there and how the décor and the architecture had changed throughout the centuries. He was impressed by the restoration and looked in wonder at the details of the four hundred year-old painted decoration, the like of which he had never seen before. But as he followed her towards, what she described as the Eighteenth Century Green Room, Duncan was aware of an overwhelming ripple of excitement down his spine, tinged with a shiver of trepidation. He paused for a moment, loosened his tie, took some deep breaths and then stepped into the room.

He looked around. He looked at the fine panelled walls. He looked at the polished floorboards, the slender furniture, and at the unknown faces watching from the gilded frames, and he thought, well what did he think? It was difficult to say really because it was all so very different, the whole house looked so very different and strangely much larger than he had imagined. But sadly he thought, 'this is all wrong, it all means nothing to me.'

'...... and this room may have been used for entertaining and showing off their best Delft China - as here....'

Duncan let the guide's voice melt into the panelled walls. Of course this was now a museum and decorated in a way that reflected the best of its history; he understood that but it wasn't what he wanted to hear or see and he wanted to shout out, 'there was no entertaining, no best china to show off and no green walls, you can't see it now but there was another story here of loss and want and deprivation.'

It was all making him feel rather uncomfortable and he was beginning to think that the visit may have been a mistake and that perhaps it was best to leave the past in its place and not interfere with it. 'It was all too long ago,' he thought, 'and maybe it would be better if I left –

'.... and you can imagine one of these ladies in the paintings sitting with her fine embroidery - just here by the fireplace...'

Duncan turned and looked at the fireplace. It had been tampered with and that bothered him. The surround had been newly plastered and streaked with white to make it look like marble. It looked bright and fresh and unused as if no hand had ever struggled to light a fire or sweep the grate. It had never looked like that.

Where were the dark trails of smoke staining the sides of the fireplace? Where were the smears of cold dirty fingers clinging to the stonework, reaching out to a smouldering fire which rarely, if ever, gave out enough heat? Where was the yelp as an unexpected spark from a piece of damp coal burst out and burnt a naked knee, a knee that was already covered in red blotches from the cold and from sitting too close to the fire in order to snatch just a little warmth? Where was the smoke filling the room and covering everything with its clinging black dust? And where was the sound of coughing? There was always the sound of coughing.

'……and glass was much cheaper by the eighteenth century so the windows were larger and there would have been a hoist just below the window ledge to bring up the large items of furniture…..'

And a rail to hang out the washing in the hope that it would dry before the smuts from the tall chimneys floated down and clung to the cloth like glue so that the whole wash needed to be scrubbed and beaten again and again by swollen red hands.

Duncan moved towards the window and looked out. Things were beginning to take shape in his mind. He looked out at the tall buildings, six, seven, eight levels high, the signature of the Old Town of Edinburgh; the world's first skyscrapers built four, five hundred years ago. Then he thought of the new buildings at home, built perhaps twenty or thirty years ago, great leviathans of glass each one reflecting the other, each one competing for the top position. He thought of the men standing on platforms hung by ropes and secured with safety harnesses, cleaning the thousands of windows, washing the glass, polishing their own reflections, seeing into the world of others high up in the sky. And then his thoughts turned to the women who once lived in these high tenements, whose flabby hips balanced precariously on narrow window ledges while they reached out with thick arms to wash their windows, wiping away the grime with just a piece of cloth, or where the glass was cracked repairing the break with a piece of newspaper that would soon be ripped off by the infernal east wind. But as the men stared into a world of strangers, these women had called out to their friends and neighbours, a shout, a laugh perhaps, or a caring word given or shared, always helping where they could.

'Aggie's bairn is due. I have to go to her. My, but she could do without another mouth to feed. I know what I would do to that man o' hers. Now where's that clean sheet? I know I put it in the press. I better take a basin as well. I wonder if Aggie has scissors.'

'Why do you need to take scissors Ma and what's her man done wrong?

'Never you mind. Now, I'll have to go. I don't know when I'll be back so I'd better take a candle as well. Now behave. There's bread on the table and some milk. I don't want to come back and hear that........'

Duncan looked down onto the courtyard. He unravelled

the seat at the top of his walking stick and eased himself on to it. It was good to rest his tired legs. It had been a long walk up to the High Street and the spiral stairs leading to this room were difficult for someone his age. But they were so easy and such fun for children.

'C'mon Andy, I'll race ye, twa steps at a time. Hurry up, Archie's gang is playing fitba.'

'Aye, I'm comin'

'Last one doon the stairs is a sissie.'

As Duncan looked out of the window, grainy images flickered before him like a silent film. Images of children playing in all weathers, some of them in bare feet, some with misshapen legs - the scourge of rickets. Boys in short trousers, girls in their mother's cut down dresses and skirts. Boys playing football, conkers or marbles. Young girls sitting in doorways looking after the bairns, the lucky few skipping to a song.

Duncan added sound to his film.

"On a mountain
Stands a lady
Who she is I do not know
All she wants is gold and silver
All she wants is a handsome beau."

A small group of children walked across the courtyard.

They were wearing brightly coloured anoraks and carrying equally bright notebooks and plastic lunch boxes. A young woman herded them into a corner out of the way of passers by. She must be their teacher, thought Duncan, how young and relaxed she looks chatting and laughing with her pupils. He smiled and then recalled a story of another Edinburgh teacher in her Prime who proclaimed that all her girls were "the crème de la crème." So many voices, so many sounds of the past. Would these carefree children learn to hear them in time?

Duncan noticed that the guide was moving in his direction. He felt that out of politeness he ought to say something and quickly looked around the room for inspiration. Furniture? China? Tapestry? No, he had nothing to say about them. What then? Maybe books? That was it. Where were the books?

'Er, I was wondering, Mam ..?'

She smiled, 'Yes?'

'I don't see any books on display.'

The guide conceded that perhaps books should be on display, because after all writers such as Scott and Burns would certainly have been read at the time.

'My mother loved Robert Burns,' Duncan said quietly,

'her favourite song was *Ae Fond Kiss.*'

' *Ae fond kiss and then we sever. Ae fareweel, and then forever ..'*

For a moment Duncan felt uneasy. Was the voice a memory, or was it an echo?

The guide, however, had warmed to the subject of the Scottish Bard.

' ….. and Robert Burns often stayed near here while he was in Edinburgh. The house is no longer there, but just where the children are sitting …….'

Duncan looked out.

'Just there?'

If only he could tell his mother. She was always singing Burns' songs while she worked and she was always working, constantly cleaning, washing, cooking, and scrubbing floors. She sang every day until the day their father died. Then the singing stopped and she had to work even harder. It was a continuous struggle to keep her family fed and clothed, and on so little money.

'Run to the shops and get a bone from the butcher, and bread - two day old bread. Here's a shilling and mind you bring back the change. Take your brother with you and don't lose him. And make sure he keeps his cap and scarf

on. He's got a bad chest the day.'

' Aye Mum.'

'Do you read Burns, Sir?'

'Yes, I have a book of Burns' poems Mam, and also the works of Stevenson and more recent Scottish authors as well. Books are my passion. I can thank my mother for that.'

'Was she a great reader?'

'No, not really, she could read of course, but she just didn't have the time and somehow … well it was a long time ago. But I guess you could say she pointed *me* in the right direction.'

The teacher stood in front of the class. She was always dressed in black and she wore black shiny boots without patches, neatly tied with strong laces. Her hair was tightly secured with pins so that no unruly curl could ever escape. She was a spinster, they were always spinsters.

'All stand now and repeat the six times table – Six ones are six, six twos are twelve .....'

Over and over again, the chant of children's voices.

Over and over again the slap, slap of the teacher's

hands as she kept the relentless rhythm, on and on and on and on.

And now after over seventy years, Duncan could still recite those times - tables. He never needed a calculator.

There was a map of the world on the wall, and a child reaching up to name the huge swathes of pink that decorated its surface. There were rows of wooden desks and children bent over black slates. There was the laborious squeaking of chalk across the surface of the slates - small letters, capital letters, words, and sentences. On the teacher's desk lying waiting for that one mistake, that slight misdemeanour, was the leather tawse....

Teachers were severe in those days unlike the young woman in the courtyard who laughed with her pupils, or the fictitious teacher who hailed her girls as the best. But he remembered that his mother was equally strict, sending her children to school in all weathers to learn their lessons, and every evening at home watching over the boys as they read and copied out long passages from library books.

.... And in the dark classroom there were the smells that would stay with you for a lifetime, smells that would catch you unawares, smells you couldn't quite define because they were everywhere, everywhere where there was a

crowd of people. It was a mixture of damp cloth, stale food and bodies. It was a smell called Poverty. And for the unlucky ones there was the additional smell of humiliation - 'there's one! and another! bring that bottle and the nit comb.' - the smell of paraffin on a child's hair when they had failed the weekly inspection. And there was the sound of coughing, always the coughing.

No-one could remain healthy living in those conditions. All those cold, damp tenements and damp clothes that never had the chance to dry out properly and in the tall, narrow closes where the sun never reached there was the constant drip, drip of water from window sills and loose guttering.

Duncan looked again at the corner by the window and thought of a young boy trying to catch the last light of day as he struggled with the words in his book and he thought of another day in a high glass tower flooded with light where an older man collected an award for journalism, commended for his great use of language.

He sensed, however, that the guide still wanted to talk.

'Where do you come from, Sir?'

'I'm from Guelph in Canada.'

'And is this your first trip to Edinburgh?'

'Well in a way, yes it is Mam.'

'Oh, in a way?

For a moment there was the awkward silence of words left unsaid.

'Er, I wonder if I may say Mam, but the story of this building seems to end around two hundred years ago. What happened then? Do you know perhaps who lived here early this century, say back in the years following the First World War?'

'Well by then Sir, this was the poorest part of town and people were living in quite desperate situations. I'm afraid, though, that real poverty is rarely noted.'

There was a smart young lady with a stiff notebook and a proper pen who would regularly come to visit various families. She would ask questions about food and clothing and coal for the fire. She would write these things down in her book. Then later some people would move out, but others would always move in and things were just the same.

'Do you have a particular interest in that time Sir?'

'Yes Mam it was my youth.'

'But things must have been so different in Canada?'

Duncan paused for a moment, and then pointed with his

walking stick.

'I would often sit by the fire just there, it was a rough wooden floor then and the fireplace looked quite - different.'

'Do you mean you lived *here*?'

'Yes Mam, in this very room with my mother, and my brother and two older sisters. But it wasn't green then, I don't remember any colour'

'You all lived in this one room?'

'Just in this one room. My brother and I slept in that corner, my sisters and mother over there. And in that other room, well I don't know how many were crowded in there.'

The guide searched for a suitable response and failed.

'My mother worked hard all the time but she just couldn't make ends meet. We all had bad chests, and there wasn't a day that one of us didn't cough.' Duncan was beginning to find the conversation difficult.

'But you moved to Canada …… '

Duncan cleared his throat,

'Yes Mam, and I became a journalist. You see, my uncle lived in Guelph. He emigrated there before we were born. After my father died he wrote to my mother saying that her two boys, myself and Andrew - not the girls, they had to stay with my mother - should go and live with him, he would pay for the passage, care for us and educate us. Our home would, henceforth, be with him in Canada. But my mother said 'No -

'She said, No?'

'I didn't quite finish, Mam. She said 'No, not until they can read and write.' You see, she may have been poor but she was rich in pride and she would only let us go to another country when we had passed our school tests in both reading and writing. Then, as she saw it, we could hold our heads high and confidently take our place with the other boys in our new country.'

'Now my wee boys, make me proud of you.'

'When we left she gave me a book of Burns' poems and she gave Andrew a copy of *Treasure Island*. She must have worked extra hard to buy them.'

'And you still have them?'

'Yes, that was the book I spoke of earlier, and my nephew now has the copy of *Treasure Island*.'

In the distance Duncan heard a door close and he looked at his watch.

'Well it sounds as if you are about to close, so I won't keep you.'

He took his last look around the room and said his goodbyes. He was glad that in the end he had left his story with the guide, the other story of the room that she may now pass on to others.

Outside once more Duncan looked back at the front of the building. How many lives had passed through that door, how many faces had peered from all those windows? His hand moved across the rough stone, 'how many stories can you tell?' he whispered, 'how many lives have you witnessed?'

After leaving the house he walked down the Royal Mile. It was still oddly familiar despite the changes; the stone setts were now much cleaner, there were cars and tourist buses instead of carts, the little dairy and the grocer shop that he remembered were now stocked with cashmere sweaters and tartan souvenirs and pubs were no longer just drinking establishments for men. He walked on passed the sombre medieval closes where groups of happy tourists were taking photographs, oblivious of the ghostly figure of a man in tight breeches visiting his clandestine lover, or the consumptive-looking man in a black velvet jacket seeking treasure. On the corner of George IV Bridge a young man with a guitar sang of the miseries of life where at one time Duncan remembered a fishwife standing with her basket of fresh herring, a basket that she had carried on her back from the shores of the Forth and up the steep hills to the Old Town. He remembered her distinctive costume; the layers of navy blue petticoats covered with a blue and white striped apron, and he remembered her musical cries:

"Bonnie fish.

Caller herrin.'

Wha'll buy my caller herrin'?"

And in his mind he saw a woman wrapped up in a thin, shabby coat looking old before her time, hurrying home to a dark tenement to ensure that her young sons learnt their lessons.

Based on a true story.

One O'Clock Gun

Giselle Mickel

You, and I,
a beautiful present,
promise.
We count on
nothing,
everything
in return.

A crack.
It is absent,
also a presence
sudden and exposed.
Its residue
confined to
ceremony.

Masquerades
as
traffic
while I climb
my black skyscraper
with spiral
stairs.

Today, bells toll.
Tomorrow,
service shall
resume
once more to signal
time spent,
lost.

That Armani Coat

Janet F Strickland

“Was that him?” Could it be? That unruly mop of wiry red hair; that coat... He used to laugh about that coat, "Okay, so it's not Armani, but it's comfortable and keeps out the rain!" She thought she saw the familiar shadowy figure reflected through the plate glass window of Samuels the Jeweller and turned quickly, but the figure was gone. Searching the sea of faces, all intent on getting home from their busy days at work she decided it must have been her imagination playing tricks on her.

Paul had been occupying her thoughts more and more since Jenny had told her he was back in Edinburgh. They hadn’t seen each other at all after leaving university, albeit they had written and sent cards a few times. They had been friends from their high school days, but it was only when they went to uni that their relationship had developed into more than that. After university he had left to work at his uncle's architect's office in London, whilst she had stayed behind and started working on the paediatric ward of the Royal Infirmary.

She turned and hurried to catch the bus home, where her thoughts took her back to the times they would drive in his old morris minor. How it had kept passing its MOT was a miracle! They would drive over to Fife and off to Perth to wander around the shops or have a picnic on the Inch, or perhaps have a day out in Portobello. How he loved that car! She reached her stop, crossed the road and made her way to her home.

"Hi mum, any messages?"

"Yes actually, Paul rang," she emphasised the last two words with a slight raise of her eyebrow. "I didn't know he was back in Edinburgh? He wanted to know if you could meet him in your "special place" around seven. So where's that then, love?" her mum asked with a grin.

"Sorry mum, must dash. Oh, and can I borrow the car please?" she added as she rushed up the stairs to shower and change. Soon after with a quick "Bye, see you later!" she jumped into the car and drove wildly through the city, as if she was a Formula 1 driver until she came to Arthur's seat. As the car snaked up and round to the car park, she looked out to their bench.

He was there.

She paused and had to stop herself from running into his open arms. “Act casually” she told herself. She allowed herself to be hugged, taking in the scent of him and feeling the all too familiar material of *that* coat!

"I see you still have this old thing then?" she smiled

"Well, It's not Armani..." he grinned back,

"...but it's comfortable and keeps out the rain," they finished together, laughing. They sat on their bench looking out over the city. It was still quite light and they could see the far shore of Fife across the Forth. The city was changing. Huge blocks of flats, built in the 1960's to re-house the people from the tenements in the poorer parts of town were being razed to the ground. Streets were being widened and many more new homes were being built. The church spires still punctuated the sky as they had for generations; the remaining high-rise flats pointing upwards, like the old mill factory chimneys. There were gaps in the buildings as a testament to all this change, with Holyrood and the other parks giving a touch of green to the scene. Edinburgh was a changing city and she wondered how much they too had changed in their time apart. Despite all that had passed between them they sat in apparent perfect harmony, each wrapped in their own thoughts as they viewed the city in the darkening shadows. However the undercurrent of things unsaid crackled between them like static electricity.

"So how have you been?" she asked eventually, breaking the silence.

Paul shifted awkwardly on the bench before turning to study her earnestly. "Okay thanks. Listen, I've been back a week already, which has just flown by, and I am sorry I didn't call you earlier. I had to give myself time to settle into my new job and find somewhere to live first." he scanned her face as if unsure how to continue. "Well now I have a great new flat in the city and I am a junior partner on a local firm of architects." he took her hand then quickly looked away. "It's getting pretty chilly; shall we go and get a coffee somewhere?"

They ordered two lattes and sat in the corner of the café on a squashy settee and Paul started tentatively talking about the future. "We both have great jobs; I have this new flat and..."

"And what?" she prompted.

"And I've missed you. If there isn't anyone else in your life just now how would you feel about starting over?"

She looked down at the ground, afraid of giving too much of herself away and not allowing herself to get too excited, recalling how she had felt the last time they parted. Was she ready to ride that rollercoaster of emotions again? To open herself up to further potential heartache if things didn't work out? But Paul took her hand and gently tilted her head up to look at him.

"This city is changing almost daily and they need new architects to rebuild it. I'm home Beth. It's where I want to be and I'd love you to share my dreams with me."

She held her breath.

"Will you marry me Beth?"

A small tear escaped from the corner of her eye which she subtly wiped away. "I'd love to marry you Paul. One day."

"But?"

"But you are just home. Shall we see how things go? It's been a while since we were together; let's give ourselves a bit of time?"

She relaxed against him as he pulled her into his arms and felt the years melt away. "There's just one thing I would ask," she whispered.

"Oh yes, what's that?" Paul replied.

"That you burn that old coat! You will soon be able to buy a real Armani that is also comfortable and keeps out the rain!"

They laughed and, hand in hand, left their cold coffees sitting untouched on the table and ran out into the darkening night.

Wrong Turning

Sarah Guppy

Pete turns off the bus engine and waits the five minutes. The bus is five minutes early and the Controller back at the Annandale Street depot appreciates punctuality. As do the customers of course. He's parked the bus at Gayfield Place, near those big Georgian houses and will resume his route after five. It is August and the whole of Edinburgh is crawling with tourists. He pulls out a paper he has stuffed behind his seat and reads the latest scandals and gossip. He's only recently got his license to drive one of these things about anyway, so better not give too much lip to anybody. But it has to be said that these vehicles deliver. He used to scoff at Lothian Bus drivers – but since he lost his job last year Pete's revised his opinion. Now he sees the amount of flak and stress they take under fire every day and he is full of admiration for them. Flak on board and flak on the road. When he'd been training he'd been warned about the weird and wonderful questions passengers may ask.

Out of the corner of his eye he spies a young lassie in a micro mini skirt – it's practically a belt, pal. Full on sexy. And it reminds him of last night, when the other half,

Audrey ranted on about him not wearing his tartan sexy-beast boxers after all the trouble she went to. It had been their anniversary and the hen was miffed. Apart from the sexy-beast shorts, he'd also forgotten to buy the commemoratory solar powered gnome. She'd almost battered him.

"Not the most romantic guy in the world are you, you bugger?" She had hissed at him. They live in a 'social inclusion zone' but never mind the regeneration of the area, thank you.

"Our bloody marriage needs to be regenerated," she had said, scowling over tea the other day, feeling very excluded. She doubted whether she could apply to some charity or partnership or even the EU to get help with encouraging Pete's active participation in their relationship. Audrey had decided they were not shagging enough. All the girls at the office where she works seem to be getting theirs. And switch on the TV or look at any mag and it is all shag this, preggie that, affair here. Pete just laughed, called her a daft hen and then had a drink. That's the way you deal with them.

A crackling sound and the Controller, Mr. McGrotty is on again. That live voice instils fear in the drivers. Better pay attention, McGrotty is ex-army. Pete stuffs the paper back and revs the big beast up again.

"Two youngsters shouting verbal abuse at driver down Leith Walk. They were thrown off, clearly drunk. About sixteen or seventeen, caps and sports gear. Over. Police informed. Please report if you see them and advise. Over. Watch your timing new drivers."

Mr. McGrotty the Controller has a wicked sense of humour and has been known to play practical jokes on new drivers. Firm but fair, you have to roll with the punches in this game. Otherwise you get more stick in the canteen and news gets round. Everyone gets the initiation treatment. Don't expect special treatment, pal. It is five twenty and Pete only started the shift at three. Another six hours or so to go. Earlier, around four-ish at the bottom of Leith Walk some bearded bookish type had climbed on board eating a carrot with a whistle hanging round his neck. *Talk about care in the community.* At least he didn't smell like some of the real nut jobs. Probably a former academic who went mad with stress. Some folk just take the piss when they hear the fares have gone up he thinks, as the bus steams along to Granton. They only put in some of the correct fare. Sometimes you can spot a skiver, a ducker and diver, like. Like last week, this Japanese tourist woman, well dressed mind, she stuffed a fiver in the box. A fiver! Pete never knew how much English they really understood. But *I'm* bloody not paid to police this too, Pete thinks. No. They want that too and they can pay me Bus Police wages.

Audrey, the missus is thinking about going back to college at nights, maybe Telford. The bus passes a slightly seedy looking tattoo shop at the top of Leith Walk. When they first started dating back in the 80s Audrey worked at the Military Tattoo selling tickets in recession ridden Old Reekie. And it was round about that time that she'd also gotten her left buttock tattooed with his name on it. Hadnae stopped her from calling him an arse though on several occasions. Not that long ago, really. Both the economy and their relationship seem to move in ever predictable repeating cycles Pete thinks, aware that he feels hungry again. Those sarnies he packed earlier got wolfed straight away. He'd chucked the crusts at a huge leering herring gull earlier in the shift at the bus depot.

"Pardon me sir, but does this bus go up to Princes Street?" Asks an American tourist who appears at the bus stop. *Sir.* I mean really. You had to laugh. The whole city swarms at this time of year: visitors are everywhere – eating ice creams, laughing at street entertainers. And that's not including those weirdo festival-arty types. He'd even seen what looked like a couple of students putting on a show in their own front room. Times must be hard. After the courteous American has hopped on board two other women, also clearly visitors, look keenly at him in the blazing late summer sun as if Pete has some special magical insight in to the workings of this city. For fuck's sake. They probably just visited the Royal Yacht. He tells them which buses they need and where to go and they look grateful. Still, at least they say please. The bus chugs right up Leith Walk. Wonder if the other half will do Shepherds Pie this evening. She is such a cracker usually. Maybe she's getting all cranky because of hormones.

It's gotten a bit overcast out there all of a sudden, changeable August weather. The bus is pretty full up now, but over the course of the shift rubbish accumulates on seats, springing up like mushrooms. Through Nicholson Street, Prestonfield and out to Niddrie and back again and now he is heading slowly back down Nicholson Street again, if the heavy traffic will let him. No sign yet of the reported abusive hoodies. A bloke in a white van pulls out way too suddenly in front of him, then gives him a load of verbal. *Ignore it pal.* Those were McGrotty's pearls of wisdom on gobby verbal abuse. When he was on training the Instructor warned him and other trainees about the down side of being a Lothian Bus driver. A troupe of drama student types with painted faces bang drums and tambourines loudly in St. Andrews Square – enough to startle pigeons and a hobo sleeping on a tastefully renovated bench. And it starts him thinking about their son John, who is doing well at the building firm – so far no black marks. They managed to wean him off the bikes and airguns at long last. After the neighbour's cat was shot at by one of John's pals they drew the line. *At sixteen, you my son, need to start taking responsibility,* they said. The watch on Pete's wrist says six thirty.

"Sorry, exact change only," Pete says politely and slowly to what sounds like some Eastern European bloke when the bus finally gets to the stop beyond St. Andrews Square. He gets the feeling he'll be saying this again and again. So far there'd been no really loud obnoxious stereos or CD players. But he can really see now how it could drive a man driving a bus up a wall. Quite literally. And these days a jam could pop up anytime – not just at so called expected peak times. *You just have to go with the flow* was what McGrotty said, in his wry sage wisdom.

Very funny, pal. His stomach is really rumbling now. The Eastern European bloke finally gets the point only after pissing everyone else off in the hot and bothered queue. Don't go there, Pete thinks. This weekend he has got to take the car in to be serviced, it's a right bummer. It will eat in to a big chunk of cash he was trying to put aside for Portugal which now seems like some distant unobtainable dream. Christ. Is three weeks ago the last time they shagged? He had been really stressed out what with the car and being a newbie on the buses. Nearly seven pm, heading back down Leith Walk again and this time it's a group of Australians. "Excuse me mate, can you tell us if you go near the Royal Yacht?" Pete assures them he goes near enough, but that it will be shut at this time.

Driving in to dimly lit Granton again, he sees Audrey has sent him a text on his mobile. He isn't allowed to have his phone switched on but she had been insistent. *Out in Cramond, don't ask. Can you pick us up.* What? He wonders which planet the other half is on. Should be a government health warning on some women. *Seriously damaging to your health, wallet and sanity.* He is really risking it now; this is only his third shift on the job like. He sees he only has one elderly couple on the lower deck and they should be no trouble. The bus is turned and steered in to Cramond and Pete gets some weird baffled looks from a couple of other bus drivers he passes – this not being his rightful route. It's a risk this, this driving out to Cramond. But then the daft hen didnae often text like this in the middle of the day. Must be important. At the bus stop Audrey is in killer black patent heels and pissed as a bat.

"Took you a long time, you bugger. Gonnae take us home, then?" she stubs out her fag and climbs on. He hints she should sit on the top deck, out of sight. The total baggage. *What the hell is she doing out in Cramond, the retired back of nowhere*. Is this a wind up or test, he thinks. *And just who does she think I am anyway – a personal chauffeur or what.* He steers the bus back to Granton but McGrotty, the All Knowing and All Powerful One has cottoned on to him. Pete should have known. The CB system crackles in to life again.

"What's happening with your vehicle, pal? Thought you'd have an away day or what? I'm getting reports that you have missed certain stops on route. Take a wrong turning or summat. Please resume your usual route asap. Report to me tomorrow morning first thing please. This cannae happen again. Over." *Shit.* He can see Audrey upstairs on the tartan CCTV laughing away. What a minx that woman is. The bus finally reaches Niddrie and he drives up Greendykes. She tumbles or half falls down the stairs.

"I'll save some Shepherds for you only if you let me have a slice of the wee fellow's action later." Pete grins. And she wasnae talkin' about the absent solar powered gnome that was for sure. Pulling away to return back to the depot and clapped out car to finish the shift Pete glances casually back in the wing mirror and sees the daft barefooted hen flashing his sexy beast shorts at him under the wee skirt she's got on. Nearly eleven thirty now. Late show visitors still throng on streets. Edinburgh's Fringe Festival seems 24 hour now. It could even border on the unhinged, this Fringe thing, Pete reckons. Years ago he had gone to one of these shows with a pal in a pub's basement. Over two pints they watched a woman making love to a chair, but had walked out half way bemused and confused, wondering if this was supposed to be what was called high brow. Four legs it seemed was more genteel than two. And to this day they remained confused as to any deeper meaning the show may have had – *their* eyebrows were still raised. But each to their own eh, at the end of the day. And seems like the earlier wrong turning has turned out alright after all he thinks, whistling and driving then in to the brightly lit depot.

An August Day

David R. Gemmell

the furnace is raging
ice-cream melting
fedora's and picnics, in
princes street gardens.

the crowd is swelling
cameras capturing memories
well-thumbed guidebooks, in
princes street gardens.

look! see the castle
look! the royal mile
hear! street performers, in
princes street gardens.

find me my island
find my retreat
let us have sanctuary, in
princes street gardens.

Voice of the Sky

Michael Flett

When I was young I called to the stars, begged the night for understanding and a place where I might belong, for the childhood promises of rockets and spaceships, astronauts and space stations, comets and shooting stars, but my cries to the sky went unheeded; the most science fiction gadget I possess is an iPhone with a cracked screen. UFOs and flying saucers haunted the deserts of New Mexico, aliens only infiltrated the suburbs, not the capital of Scotland.

For over two hundred years, Edinburgh has hosted an observatory, originally built on Calton Hill and given royal appointment by George IV in 1822, but science moves swiftly; to use an aphorism of that discipline, it evolves. Early ideas are superseded, the very tools by which the art is performed and their practitioners cast aside, dismissed and forgotten. If a name defines a thing, gives it purpose, maybe even grants it power, how long does that meaning last when the reason that name was bestowed no longer applies?

I know the ancients watched the sky with nothing more than their eyes and brains, yet with the sophistication of those tools they charted the movements of wandering bodies against the firmament, a name indicating permanence, that the stars are fixed and unchanging. With their telescopes, enlightenment astronomers gave identities to the planets beyond the mythological attributes of their classical names, and soon the stars were no longer dismissed as points on a crystal sphere in which the Earth hung central; they too had personalities and traits, births and deaths.

The relocation of the observatory to Blackford Hill took place on the cusp of the twentieth century, in the same year as HG Wells wrote his famous tale of Martian invasion, less than a decade before cinematic pioneer Georges Méliès turned his camera lens to Jules Verne's fantastical account of a trip to the moon, creating the first ever science fiction film, the first of many broken promises of humanity's future in the stars.

Our world is turbulent and unstable, spinning off kilter and dragging the atmosphere behind it, hurtling around the sun in an echo of the swirling disc of matter that formed the solar system, the plates of crust grinding against each other as hot rock oozes between cracks and cools to form new mountain ranges under the sea; on the surface the sun blasts down, the radiation released back to the sky at lower wavelengths at dusk.

The cold twinkling of the night sky that entrances the casual observer is the air rippling as heat dissipates into space, but the effect renders any information contained therein useless; altitude and atmospheric stability are the overriding factors in practical stargazing, and while this grand edifice may have stood against the horizon of the Athens of the North for over a century, it has passed into history as surely as that ancient city, any achievement overshadowed by the remote mountain peak observatories with which it could not compete.

By the mid-twentieth century, even as satellite launches and the space race turned all eyes towards the heavens, astronomy had been pushed out of the cities by the sodium glow that washed out the ancient illumination of the pale Milky Way. The advent of radio astronomy meant the universe could be hesitatingly grasped, if not yet fully comprehended, but that advancement did not happen on this lonely hill. The isolation of Jodrell Bank in England and Aricebo in the more exotic Puerto Rico advanced the new astronomy. Visible light astronomy had told us all it could tell us, was now a pastime strictly for amateurs, for dabblers. We no longer look at the sky; we are now listeners, not observers.

Within the last generation, all ground-based work was made redundant by the Hubble and its cousins whose lofty positions afford privilege incomparable, illuminated veils of gas and dust crowding before their lenses, whole galaxies revealed, back thirteen billion years to the edge of forever. With the majesty of the night unmasked by its descendants, the Royal Observatory adjusted to that role reserved for all of us who have suffered the indignity of outliving our usefulness, and it became a teaching centre, tracking asteroids and occasionally registering the discovery of a new block of frozen rock to add to overflowing catalogues.

And so it remains, a monument in a city crammed with those, as much a historical artefact as the precious tomes of the extensive library it houses, among them early editions of those whose names are still commemorated in astronomy as craters on the moon, Tycho Brahe, or space probes and orbiting instruments, Nicolaus Copernicus, Johannes Kepler and Galileo Galilei, even the man who deciphered the fundamental laws of motion, Isaac Newton. Together, they offered us the stars.

I look up at the copper domes that conceal the telescopes and try to connect myself with that wonder, to find my place in this vast and glorious universe, but I am trapped in flesh; the elements in my body may have been forged in the atomic fire of ancient supernovae, but I was cast out. The Old Testament parallel is not lost on a rational sceptic like me, and I smile, but only because the alternative, as Heinlein pointed out, would be to weep.

Life changes, but the stars do not on any time scale a human can witness. In the time required for a volcano to wash away or a continent split apart, in those terms, stars will live a fraction of their lives, shift position as they dance in each other's gravity, breathe fire and light out into the cosmos, spewing out energy and rare elements when they reach their catastrophic deaths. But in the space of a human life, the sky does not speak. We listen, but the sky does not grace us with meaning or insight other than what we can discern indirectly. And if the stars watch us, they are indifferent. When Carl Sagan said, "We are a way for the cosmos to know itself," the words felt important, but tonight my uncertainty overwhelms his calm assurance of the importance of my species.

The mariners of old used the stars to guide them from

port to port, farmers sowed crops and managed their livestock by the season, but with concrete around us, each dwelling uniform with those that flank it, pedestrian crossings herding us like animals, the glare of street lights banishing night, I wonder whether, in giving up the sky, have we lost our way? Have we voluntarily become statistics, unquestioning consumers trapped on an endless battle to keep the economy afloat?

Arthur C Clarke, the man who first conceived global communication, said his worst decision was to allow a fax machine into his home, and he wisely refused an email account, aware that we have little to say to each other. In letters we once revealed ourselves, considered and described our deepest thoughts, but the immediacy of electronic messaging requires no such contemplation; we tweet vacuous proclamations, stripped of punctuation or grammar. When we still slaughter the grand inhabitants of the jungles and oceans, I doubt whether the ability to broadcast our vanity across the oceans made us a better species.

And so on this soft evening I stand on the wide driveway and look out across the static city, witness to distant street lights and roving headlights, the noise of traffic rising from below. The lights are hard and unwavering, their constancy marking them as unnatural. Where once there was grass and forest, now there is concrete. Life is an infection that spreads across the surface of the planet, endlessly consuming and polluting that which sustains it with toxins that are its inevitable by-product.

The changing sky remains a constant reminder of possibility. Out west, the sun has dipped below the Pentlands, ripples of crimson and cerise echoing on the sparse clouds, bidding farewell to the dying summer day. On the other horizon, the peak of Arthur's Seat still catches the sun, but its slopes are in shadow. I can just catch the movement of walkers, dark specks against the rocks; the sky behind is falling to darkest blue as the sun sinks.

The story goes that the inspiration for Jules Verne's *Vingt Mille Lieues Sous Les Mers* was a very wet walking holiday in Scotland, not that I'm familiar with any other kind. In his mind, the volcanic landscape transposed to the seabed, the Acropolis on Calton Hill, where the Observatory was sited during his visit, imagined as the ruins of Atlantis, the welcoming dining room window of his host glimpsed through sheets of rain becoming the illuminated porthole of the Nautilus. Verne and Wells, fathers of science fiction: as day turns to dusk, surely I cannot be the only lonely disciple who waits for the bright future you envisioned?

The rock beneath my feet is older than recorded history, a fragment expelled by the churning innards of the planet, weathered stump of a volcano, colder than the evening air. Mineral fragments sparkle within as my gaze shifts, capturing the street lights and casting them back at me, mocking the lack of stars above. I had hoped the sky would have darkened sufficiently for hints of the constellations to emerge before I had to leave, but it is time to go.

Gravel crunching beneath my bicycle, I push off towards the downward winding path. The noise is firm and satisfying, the wind in my hair an affirmation of movement, a justification of my presence. I consciously leave my melancholy behind me, where it belongs. This is an occasional indulgence, a place of history where I can consider and reflect before the time comes to move forward again. Like the dusty tomes of lore on those shelves, I seal my past and failures within the pages of a book that few will open.

The modest dwellings of suburbia slide past, giving way to larger buildings that rise and steal the sky, heavy traffic, smokers gathered outside bars, the sounds of weekend night life, louder than the silent voice of the sky. Approaching The Meadows, a red light stops me, and I take the opportunity to look up: Vega, purest white, dazzles overhead, unmistakable; my eyes track swiftly to the positions of Deneb and Altair, locating them without difficulty as my eyes adjust, the summer triangle suspended above me. For all the distance between us, some friends are more reliable than others. Buoyed on by their reassuring presence, the lights signal me onwards.

A car belches past in the other direction, trailing a black miasma like a *Flash Gordon* rocket ship sans the slick chrome exterior. The sandwich board outside a newsagent warns of rising waters, and I remember Wyndham cautioning us fifty years ago that the floods would push humanity back to the hills, and now his storm is gathering. If thirty years ago we had invested in researching wind and wave power instead of drilling the North Sea, we would have been world leaders by now, instead of scrabbling at the heels of the paymasters of the Big

Smoke.

For all its changes, I am still proud to have been born in this city, though I pedal through the streets as an alien, unrecognised, each year adding wrinkles and cynicism. I see in the distance the torches are burning on the walls of the castle, flickering into the evening, the battlements floodlit in blue light from the esplanade where the Tattoo seating has been set up. It's a perfect night for it, still warm and cloudless, no threat of rain. Thirteen and a half billion years it has taken to arrive at this moment, whether by random chance or covert direction, does it matter? This is where we are.

As I coast towards George IV Bridge, I anticipate the sight that will greet me on the High Street, entertainers, jugglers, buskers, touts offering free passes to their midnight comedy revues, dancers performing routines on the cobbles for any who will stop a moment. I have sufficient time to pass by Cockburn Street for a baked potato, veggie haggis with butter and black pepper, enjoy the spectacle before I have to be at Charlotte Square.

Later tonight, Banks is talking about the technological star-spanning meta civilisation known as the Culture, but I have this bit of culture in the meantime. Last night there were two girls in miniskirts singing arias by St Giles; in front of the council chambers, a flamenco guitarist. By the Tron Kirk, the blues ruled, ironic counterpoint to the ghost tour that sauntered past as I listened.

Is it any wonder you can lose yourself, when this is what your city does best, constantly recreating itself, metamorphosing into a vast stage and inviting anyone who wishes to perform, participate or just observe. The summers may be brief, but we fill them well, and we have other stars now. In past years I've had a smile from Sigourney, given thanks to Tilda, talked Timelords with Gaiman and Browncoats with Brookmyre. What tonight will bring, tomorrow, next year…

I tell myself that I should travel more, but the curse of this bustling city is the vibrancy which lures you in, captures you with the promise that if you wait long enough, everything you can imagine will come to you instead. Tonight, I'm ready for whatever fate the stars offer me.

The sudden crackle of gunfire above causes me to look up, and the sparkle of fireworks radiates out across the sky, the sizzle and glitter of igniting titanium and magnesium powders, the powerful green of barium chloride and yellow of sodium nitrate, and for that moment I am a child again, entranced by the simple chemistry of wonder. For a moment, fading from the sky even as I conceive the thought, these stars have been made just for me.

Journey's End

Andy Nairn.

A steady drizzle continues to lubricate the road, making the lights glare sickly yellow from every surface. People huddle under umbrellas as they make their way out of the city after another gruelling day of corporate servitude and office politics. There seem to be no happy people here in the dank misery of Edinburgh's offices and middle class town houses.

At last, I have negotiated the route to the "Conan Doyle". I don't know if Sir Arthur ever graced the place, to me it's the place I turn right to get up to Princes St. The road is tarmac, a welcome relief from the bone juddering cobbles, although half of this road is given over to buses and taxis so I drive up the right hand lane until I'm nearly at the top then switch into the left lane so that I can get across Princes Street and turn left onto North Bridge and drive over the glass parapets of Waverley Railway Station.

A bus pulls past in its own lane and as usual no faces appear at the windows, filthy with road spray and foul biodiesel fumes. Crossing the bridge, it stops at an empty shelter, to wait for its appointed slot on the "Integrated Transport" timetable. A taxi wallows in the buses' wake, the driver searching for a break in the traffic in the “everyone else” lane to pull out and pass the bus. A harried looking passenger in a suit gawkes out the side window.

The double decker bus can barely make it up the hill, and has to stop again. No-one gets on or off the bus, it just has to stop, rules. A cloud of smelly black diesel fumes cover the taxi when the bus pulls away and the air smells vaguely of burnt chip fat.

I'm in the lane with all the rest of the cars, patiently waiting as the queue lurches forward a few car lengths every time the lights at the Royal Mile change in our favour.

Onward we lurch into the night, smooth tarmac glistening in the moonlight and car lights. The taxi engine roars as the driver tries to move out of the bus and taxi lane to merge into the everyone else lane, but we're having none of it, like elephants protecting our young we present an unbroken line of steel that he is unable to penetrate with his cab nose.

The bus finally moves off and the taxi gives up his attempt in favour of following the bus up to the lights.

The Royal Mile. Scotland's kings were never crowned here. This is the seat of English oppression of the Scots from ancient times. Murderer's and thieves were hanged here alongside those who dared to think for themselves. Covenanters, Jacobites and those who understood the healing properties of herbs, or just lived beside a mad neighbour who accused them, were brutalised, and finally killed as witches on this ancient approach to the Castle.

At last I can see the theatre ahead of me on the right, so I need a place to park my car. I look at the clock on the dash, six thirty, perfect, since street parking is free from this very moment. A break in the steady stream of umbrella toting pedestrians, a cobbled speed bump on the left, I turn in to Drummond Rd and passing the Hispaniola pub on the left and the takeaway on the right I find an empty parking space next to a cardboard recycling bin. A deft parking manoeuvre and I turn the key to enjoy the quiet of the car for a moment and gather my thoughts.

Next time I'll take the train and walk here, it's much quicker than using the car, or a taxi, but I'll never be on one of those huge, empty, smelly buses.

The door has a "Cool Place To Be" sticker on it, and I have to agree.

Spoon Bistro is warm, and the friendly atmosphere is exemplified by the man serving.

"Can I have the chicken dish, and a mug of cappuccino?"

"Certainly, where will you be sitting?"

"With the writer's club, at the bench by the window."

I'm the first here, so I settle myself into one of the many leather arm chairs, take out my tablet and start typing a short story while I'm waiting for the others to arrive.

Another Mary

Janette Crawford

I've just had some awful news. My brother Robert has just been in to tell me that the Queen is dead. Beheaded! And that the death warrant was signed by her own cousin, Queen Elizabeth in London. That's a terrible way to die and after all those years spent as a prisoner first in that small place in the middle of Lochleven and then in all those castles in England. The poor thing tried so hard for her freedom, but she had just too many enemies, and there were too many people that didn't care, aye, even here in Scotland. Rob works at the Royal Mews in Holyrood and he hears all these things.

It seems no time at all since I saw her arrive in Leith. I was only a wee girl then, but it was a day that I'll never forget and I don't think it's too much to say that the events of that day changed my life. I remember the haar was hanging around dripping like wet washing, which was unusual enough for August, but that morning it was so bad that you could scarce see a person in front of you. Great bulky shapes would suddenly appear from nowhere then disappear just as quickly through the mist, just like ghosts, except ghosts wouldn't swear out loud as those apparitions did when they bumped into a wall or tripped o'er an abandoned creel.

I've always been fascinated by haar and the way it's never static, but drifts along in waves, one minute looking like the tattered remnants of an old sail and the next covering everything just like a great white woolly blanket. I used to love standing by the river, lost in its mist, hearing only the creaking of the rowlocks and the slurping of the tide against the sodden steps or listening to the warning calls of disembodied voices on the ships. Then when the haar cleared and everything took shape again, there was the deafening shriek of gulls fighting for fish. That's what the haar does, it plays with your senses just like being in a dream.

Well that morning I had to go to the bakehouse with some dough for the oven. My mother had wrapped it up in a cloth and put it in my basket, then she wound me up in her old rough shawl to keep out the chill. On the way I kept close to the walls of the buildings to try and avoid folk, but I was so small they didn't see me and would bump into my basket. Then I would get yelled at as if it was all my fault.

I noticed that the quayside seemed busier than usual

that day with small groups of finely dressed men all huddled together, and I overheard one of them say that John Knox had called the awful weather a bad omen for Scotland. That was John Knox the minister at St Giles' up in the High Street in Edinburgh. I had heard it said that he was always angry in the Kirk and thumping the pulpit during his sermons. Somebody even said he flew out of the pulpit in a rage - a frightening image for a young lass and probably why I remember it.

Another man said that this was a very poor welcome for her Majesty. Her Majesty! Ah well, I did know something about this because, like most children, I liked to listen in to the older folk's conversations, and there had been talk of the Queen returning to Edinburgh from France. Why did I remember this? Well because the Queen had the same name as me - Mary. I tugged at the sleeve of the man nearest to me and asked him what was happening.

'We're waiting for the ship that's bringing the Queen back to rule in Scotland,' he said.

I remember that he paused for a moment and looked far out into the mist.

'There will be a lot of changes now and not all for the better.'

‘Is that why John Knox is angry,’ I replied.

He looked down at me.

‘What could you know about it? Be off with you, the ship will be here any minute.’

Well I’d never seen a Queen before so I wasn’t going anywhere. I crouched down by the side of a wall to wait, tucking my feet into my skirt to keep them warm and out of everybody’s way, and completely forgetting about the bakehouse.

I didn’t have too long to wait before the outline of a great galley cut through the mist. It looked in a really sorry state with its damp sails hanging like shrouds across its mast. Then all of a sudden it thumped against the quay, the main mast swayed, and there was a yell as a sail came loose and started to unravel. A rope came flying through the air and somebody shouted, ‘catch it,’ but that was difficult because nobody could see it.

The commotion attracted the seagulls and they came swooping and circling about our heads, bawling and laughing the way they do, and I took the chance and jumped up from my hidey-hole and pushed passed all the people to get as close to the ship as I dared.

It was a few minutes before anything happened, but

then from out of the mist emerged a very tall lady. She was dressed in a black dress with a little black hat on her red hair. Red hair, just like mine! On the quayside all those fine men moved forward and bowed in front of her and I heard them murmur, 'Your Majesty,' but they were blocking my view and somehow I just had to get near to the Queen of Scots because I remembered that our neighbour Jenny Cunningham had said - she was a great one for stories and for telling fortunes - she said that it was good luck to touch the dress of a queen. I thought of my poor mother and the one shabby room that she and my brother and I lived in, its leaking roof, the dark and the cold and the midden outside. We could do with some good luck. So I squeezed and pushed my way between the legs of the gentlemen and reached the front just as the tall lady Queen stepped ashore. I stretched out my hand and just caught the cloth at the back of her dress. It was so soft and sleek. I had never felt anything like it in my life. It was like stroking the soft fur on a cat's tummy. But just as I had it between my fingers, somebody pushed me and my cold feet slipped on the slimy ground. My basket went one way, and the bread dough the other but I did manage to keep hold of the hem of the Queen's dress to steady myself.

The Queen felt the tug and looked around to see what had happened and then she saw me. I looked up to her, all the way up, and felt my heart thump, thump in my chest. She said something to one of the ladies beside her, but her voice sounded strange to me, sort of like music, that's the only way I can describe it. I couldn't understand any of the words. Then she bent down towards me. Just in time I let go of the hem of her dress and tucked my hands into my shawl. Well, she touched the side of my face with the back of her hand and then held my chin for a few moments. Her hands were so slender and soft. I had never experienced the like of them before. My poor mother's hands were always so red and rough and chapped.

'You poor thing, you look so cold and wet,' she said.

I understood her now and thought that the spoken word had never sounded so sweet. Thinking back, I must have looked quite a sight, with my wet hair hanging around my face and my feet covered in grime, but at the time I didn't care. She asked my name and when I replied, 'Mary', she laughed and said 'Ah, another Mary' although she pronounced it *Maree*. Then she turned and spoke to her ladies for a few minutes and they rummaged in their bags and in the pockets of their cloaks as if they were looking for something.

By this time the men by the quayside were becoming annoyed and one of them started shaking his fists at me, but the Queen ignored them and turning back to me gave me a little cloth purse made of the same material as her dress. On the front it had the tiniest, most perfect embroidery stitches in the shape of a yellow flower. Inside the purse I felt something round and hard but before I could open it, or even thank her, I was pushed out of the way and the Queen was led to Mr Lamb's house around the corner. The little purse had a long cord so I put it round my neck and tucked it inside my shawl. It was only then that I noticed my basket rolling around the quayside - empty - and a gaggle of seagulls fighting over the dough.

I knew that my mother must be anxious about me so I grabbed the empty basket and ran home. I burst in, but before she could draw breath to shout at me I told her everything, all about the people and the ship and about seeing the Queen, and then I gave her the purse. She opened it and I still remember her face, it was so pale as she took out a large shiny gold coin. Her voice was a whisper, 'Oh Mary this will feed us for weeks, maybe months. Oh I've never seen the like o' it.' She sat down on her little stool with her hand covering her mouth and I remember that her shoulders were shaking.

Well, Jenny Cunningham certainly seemed to know what she was talking about because things started to get better after that. My brother got a job mucking out the stables at Holyrood and soon after that my mother got a job as a servant to a rich lady who lived in one of the tall houses in Edinburgh. I was allowed to go with her and we slept in a bed in the kitchen, which was much better than many servants had, and the glow from the big fire kept us warm on winter's nights. The lady took quite a fancy to me and in between my chores she taught me how to read and write and it was such a wonder to me to see all the letters joined up to make the words I used every day.

We lived with her for a few years until she died. We then had to move up to one of the small attic rooms, but at least it was our own home and by then I had a job as a seamstress so I was able to look after my mother. I also began to keep a journal, writing down my thoughts and my memories and when I had time I would sit by my window and write about the people I could see way down in the High Street.

And this is where you've found me now, writing in my

journal, but with the saddest heart. I still have the little purse the Queen gave me all those year's ago, it's quite worn now and the yellow stitches have faded, but I would never part with it. I keep it wrapped in a piece of linen in my sewing box. What a clever needlewoman she was. Funny to think that's what I do now.

I'm told that the two Queens never met. But when I think back to what Jenny Cunningham said, and then about my family's good fortune, well I can't help thinking that perhaps if they had met, and Mary had touched Elizabeth's dress, maybe that would have brought her better luck and she would have lived a longer and happier life.

Libberton Wynd

Andy Nairn

There it was, calling to her. He was bragging about it, showing it to his friends and pointing out the various "apps" he had installed. Jacky could see the screen change colour as he tapped it with the tip of his finger, but at least she was spared him stepping through all the ringtones. It was one of the new smart phones, just on the market, so it would fetch a good price from Dave in the phone repair shop. Jacky marked out her target. The man dropped the phone back in his jacket pocket before pushing through the crowd to get to the bar. She walked over and brushed against his jacket, carelessly hung over the back of a chair, and reached into his pocket, gently slipped her fingers around the slim plastic box and moved it to her own pocket in one deft move. She carried on walking, picking other jacket pockets and handbags left open by careless clients of the pub as she went, working her way down the stairs and around the dance floor.

All was going as planned until the phone erupted in a blast of Van Halen's "Jump" and lit up through the pocket of her shell suit. Jacky looked at the owner of the phone, he was looking straight back at her first looking puzzled, then his face flushed red as he realised what was happening and he began to shout and wave his arms in an attempt to attract the attention of his friends and the doorman..

"Hey! That's my phone!" He tried to chase her, but he was three deep in the crowd at the bar and the best he could manage was to point, "Get her!"

The bouncer at the door, a bald, thick necked man who didn't fit the athlete mould, was looking around trying to see who the man at the bar was pointing at. Jacky saw all this in a second, panic had changed her perception and everything was going in slow motion. On reflex she started to run barging through the crowd, spilling drinks and knocking people into each other, pushing her way past the bouncer, evading his hands by ducking past his belly and almost falling into the street.

She was in Grassmarket, a broad pedestrian area of the old town, and heading down the hill over cobbles with the noise of outrage rising in her wake. She was conspicuous in her metallic blue shell suit and although she was dressed for running in her trainers, her lifestyle of cheese and chips, cider, and cigarettes was not athletic. The din of people shouting and giving chase increased behind her.

She reached Cowgate, above her the George IV bridge towered casting the street into shadow in the light of the full moon. Jacky stopped under the bridge gasping for breath. Her heart was racing and she could hear the blood pulsing in her ears. Too much cider and fags was taking its toll. She walked on through the arch trying to catch her breath.

The sound of shouting suddenly grew louder. Someone was running towards her, hard shoes slipping and scuffing on the slick cobbled surface.

Jacky had to get out of sight, find some cover. She spotted a dark alcove in deep shadow, offering a spot of inky blackness which would hide her conspicuous shiny clothes. She ran into the alcove, pressing her back against the door it concealed. It swung open silently and she fell through the doorway. Scrambling backwards until her feet were inside, Jacky was relieved to have discovered this hiding place, the door quietly closed with a click. Jacky was surrounded in complete darkness. It felt palpable, like a blanket constricting her breathing. She gasped short, shallow breaths, listening for her pursuer, but all she could hear was the racing of her pulse and her wheezing as she fought for each breath of the damp, musty air.

There was no noise of hard shoes on road on the other side of the door, but Jacky was not ready to take the chance of stepping back into the moonlight just yet. She pulled herself up against the wall and waited for the pain in her chest and arm to subside.

No cigarettes, she could just go a fag too.

Her sweat dripped into her eyes, stinging, but she couldn't wipe it away, her hand wouldn't move.

***

Jacky awoke with bright sunlight stabbing at her eyes and the noise of shouting filling her head with confusion, but it was the smell which told her immediately that something was wrong.

She watched a crow glide to the ground and land with a single flap of midnight wings on the corpse of a rat. Jacky watched in horror as it dug out the rat's eyes with the point a razor sharp beak. The bird looked up at her, turning its head, and that blood covered beak to one side and then the other, then its black wings opened and lurching towards her. It took off and flew over her head with a gust of fetid odour and screeching. The smell was overpowering, like walking into the toilet after your dad came out. Jacky followed the crow as it flew towards Grassmarket until her attention was drawn by a man in a felt hat.

“Aye it's strong the day lass,” the man in fancy dress was standing across the end of a narrow street looking quizzically at her, “Ge'in ye the boak is it?”

Down the middle of the narrow street flowed a stream of brown sludge. Lumpy and foul, it oozed out onto the cobbled street like the ichor of death where it joined a small river of similar lumpy, smelly soup.

Jacky looked at the man in fancy dress, he seemed odd, and it wasn't just the costume.

“Nicol Mushet,” he removed his black felt hat and bowed deeply, “I am the Laird of Boghall.”

Jacky was still disoriented, but the fog was lifting and she realised this man wanted an answer. Best to go along with the local loonies or they can turn nasty, she thought.

“Jacky,” she said trying to shake the fog out of her thoughts. “Fancy dress last night ?”

A short, petite woman walked up behind Mushet, shouting at him all the while. She too was in fancy dress, a fine blue gown with white petticoats and club heel shoes.

“Aye! Tryin to put it about are ye ?” She prodded him roughly in the chest and turned to Jacky.

“Ye'd best be getting along noo, we're no wantin' your sort about here ya hussy.”

The woman turned back to Mushet raising her voice in a constant stream of oaths and curses, prodding him in the chest. A blade flashed in Mushet's hand. Slashing at the woman's neck, it struck creating a fountain of blood.

The woman gurgled as she fell, her scream lost in drowning and foaming blood on the flagstones where it mixed with the brown stream.

Jacky put her hands over her face, hiding from the horrific sight, the gruesome gurgling of Mushet's victim.

“Aye ye'll no nag me now wife. I paid with my life for a moment of anger. Hangin on the gibbet at the top o Libberton Wynd till my life drained out of me as your blood drains from you.”

Half expecting to see a knife slash towards her Jacky peered through the gaps in her fingers, but the man was gone and the body of the woman had disappeared along with the blood. The crow watched her from the gutter of the building opposite, before launching itself on those evil looking black wings and lazily flapped up the street between the houses.

A noise assaulted her ears, and pulling her hood back

she stood up to see what it was.

Unfortunately the stench remained, and the noise grew louder as a cart approached up the cobbled street, pulled by a burly man. He ignored Jacky as he passed, straining as he pulled his heavy cart up the narrow street, his naked feet treading in the oozing stream and splashing his tatty canvas trousers.

The cart was covered with a tarpaulin, and Jacky wondered what he could be hauling.

The cart bumped over the edge of a flagstone in the street and an arm slipped from beneath the tarpaulin.

"Bring out yer dead!" shouted the man. He stopped and put down the cart handles, then pulled back the tarpaulin.

Death!

The smell was overpowering. Swollen, naked, bodies with gaping mouths were piled up in the cart, thrown there with no respect for who they once were or the things they had achieved. The man stopped at a door with a white cross marked on it. The door opened and a girl lay there dead, naked, cold in the doorway. Her lips were black and blood was crusted around her eyes and ears. The man hefted her onto his cart and threw the tarpaulin over her, but her head hung below it's edge and her gaping eyes stared coldly at Jacky, her mouth wide in a silent scream. Jacky bent double and wretched, adding the contents of her stomach to the putrid, stinking stream.

"Good day to you."

Jacky stumbled for words to reply to the middle aged man in fancy dress who was holding his hat above his head.

"Yeah... hello"

There was something just a bit odd about the man but Jacky couldn't put her finger on it, apart of course from his medieval get up. The man put his hat back on his head and looking her up and down again, scowled and walked off up the street.

Two particularly ugly looking women were walking down the street pushing a man in front of them. Both women were wearing long dresses, but their short hair looked out of place and their voices were Bonnie Tyler deep. “Aye save yer own neck James Brown !” shouted one of the women as she punched the man in the back with a big hairy fist.

“Am sorry George, Willie.” The other woman slapped him across the face and James reeled.

“Sorry'll no help ye Jimmy.”

"We had got away with it." George prodded James with his thick finger, "We had five thousand outa that coach and the polis were lookin fur three women till you dropped us in it."

"Aye and then ye get off free by lettin us hang! Ya wee ..." George turned and looked at Jacky.

"Whit're you lookin at ?" Jacky fumbled for words but none came. "At least ah look mare like a wummin than you !" He held her gaze for a moment before turning his ire back on James and the three walked off, tussling, towards Grassmarket.

The buildings on either side of the street were tall, and looked haphazard with windows and doors facing in all directions, balcony windows overhanging the rough, uneven flagstones and cement of the street. It was quite busy now, with women and small children walking barefoot in their tatty clothes, picking their way around the filth. None of them paid her any attention as she made her way slowly up the street which was odd because she was dressed so differently.

There was a grand looking stair case some way up the street, and so used to being ignored was Jacky that she stopped short when a clean looking woman shouted to her from the staircase.

"Come on up here lass, I'll get you good business. Mary McKinnon will look after ye." The woman wore a green silk dress with white petticoats and long sleeves. She had a knife in her hand, blood dripping from the tip.

At the top of the street was a pub, "Burns Tavern". Surrounded by the miasma of vomit and urine, the walls were stained yellow. Across from the pub a well dressed man sat in the doorway, Jacky assumed it wasn't his doorway since that would likely be in an altogether nicer part of town. He was smoking a long clay pipe, with an aroma that reminded her of her grandfather, when she used to visit him on Sundays. At the time she had hated those visits, dragged by her mother, always fighting and throwing tantrums, then sulking in the corner, but all the time listening to their every word.

The man looked directly at her. "You're new, what's your name?" Jacky had a reflex "Who sir me sir?" moment.

"Yes, you in the shiney clothes."

"Jacky, Who're you?"

"I'm the infamous postmaster Thomas Urquate, caught

stealing money from the letters." She wondered what that had to do with him hanging out at a dive in some fancy dress costume from Edinburgh's smelly past.

"Ah! You don't understand." The postmaster threw her an inquisitive look. "You must be very new."

"Yes, I'm very new here, wherever here is"

"This dear girl is Libberton Wynd, one of the most famous streets in the city." He pointed the stem of his pipe down the stinking narrow street. "That street at the top is Lawnmarket, the gallows of the common man, and down at the bottom is Cowgate and Grassmarket with the lockup for the condemned."

"I recognise the names, but not the places, or the people, and they all dress like in a history book, and they all ignore me."

"Yes it is confusing at first. I don't think the ordinary people can see us, but we can see each other." He gave Jacky a quizzical look and pointed his pipe at her. "What do you call those ?" Jacky looked down at her blue shiny clothes. Urquate was the only one who had remarked on them, which considering the garb of the rest of the people she had seen was a bit surprising.

"It's a shell suit, athletes wear them."

"Are you an athlete?" If she was, then athletics must have changed a lot, thought the postmaster.

"No," Jacky would have been embarrassed if she knew how, "it's fashion."

"Ah French. That explains it."

"I'm not French. I live in Lothian Road, just up from the arcade." He looked blank, as if he was trying to figure out some foreign language.

"Not any more dear girl, you're one of us now."

***

Two women sat in front of the coal effect of Edwina's electric fire. The house had central heating but the coal effect looked warm. The walls were yellow, but that wasn't the colour of the paint. The TV blared lunchtime news in the corner, pushing its picture through clouds of cigarette smoke.

"The body of the woman was found by a caretaker here at the National Library of Scotland who was checking the fire exits this morning. Police say the cause of death has not yet been established." The reporter stood under a black umbrella with the George IV bridge in the background. There was police tape and two men in green overalls pushing a black plastic bag on a trolley between them.

Jacky's mother slurped the tea from her mug, stubbed out her fag end, and turned to her friend.

"See that Sadie?" Sadie screwed up her face conspiratorially and nodded before slurping her own tea.

"Bet I know what she was doing up that fire exit."

Their cackling stopped short when the doorbell rang, and Jacky's mother could make out the outline of two police uniforms through the frosted glass in the door.

She pulled the door open till it was stopped by the chain. "What's she been up to this time then ?"

"Mrs Edwina Collins ?" The policewoman couldn't have been much older than Jacky. "Can we come in, we have to talk to you."

Edwina closed the door to take the chain off, shouting "Sadie, the police are here. That girl has been up to no good again."

***

Urquate smiled at Jacky with a glint in his eye. "My dear, you are stuck here with those punished for their crimes on the gallows of Liberton Wynd."

The Two Williams

Eliza Keating

Here's the story of a gruesome pair
one named Burke and other named Hare.
From Ireland coast made their retreats
and ended up on our fair streets.
In Tanners - a lodging place
two Williams first came face to face.
soon a friendship these men struck
what a piece of utter ghastly luck.

Both of them able and more than willing
anything they'd do to make a quick shilling.
By chance,
shared their abode with an auld army gent
who selfishly died without paying his rent.
£4 he had owed before he off and went
Retrieving the money the pair were hell bent.

Down by Canon Gate in auld reekies wynds,
studied doctors and surgeons with medical minds.
Only corpse they could get were men from the gallows
souls never buried in ground that was hallowed.
One surgeon called Knox would turn a blind eye,
fresh bodies from graves the doctor would buy.
So Burke said to Hare, or did Hare say to Burk,
lets no bury this body in auld Canongate kirk

Down Edinburgh streets cobbled and narrow
took old man's remains in a rusty wheel barrow.
Sold him to the doctors down at Surgeons Square,
who dissected his corpse with a cut and a tear.
So by earning themselves such a handsome tally,
they decided no longer to dilly or dally,
wouldn't wait for death by natural means.
The pair decided they must intervene.

Enticing their victims with booze filled glass'
always careful to pick from the under class'.
So drunk were their prey had no strength to fight
the cads smothered them dead in the still of the night.
Then off they'd swagger to Surgeons Hall
with the seventeen bodies they murderd in all.
For each cadaver their palms were well greased
Courtesy of course of the newly deceased.

Now is often the case and often the trend
sadly all good things must come to an end.
And it happened to them one Halloween night,
when a lodger of theirs got a terrible fright.
Annie Grey found a body, right under her bed
and straight to the police, wee Annie soon fled.
And in Edinburgh town they all held their breaths
till the two were caught for these untimely deaths.

Of course Hare blamed Burke and Burke blamed Hare.
Each blaming the other for the putrid affair.
Hare being more cunning had an ace up his sleeve,
if it worked would earn him a hasty reprieve
turned his evidence showed allegiance to king,
knowing that left only Burke there to swing.
So thus sparing his neck from the hangmans knot,
but just for a moment lets give them a thought.

So did crafty old Hare pay for his crime?
Well a crowd tossed him into a pit full of lime.
The lime burned at his eyes right into the sockets,
left a blind beggar man not a penny in pockets.
You would think here lies the end of their story
But no, there are things yet even more gory.
For it seemed only fitting and somehow quite fair
they returned old Burke's body back to Surgeons Square.

In front of a crowed that all clapped and cheered,
dissected the man that all Edinburgh feared.
Put in a glass case he still stands there today,
as a constant reminder that crime doesn't pay.
Well that was the story of the infamous pair.
Two irish rogues,William Burke,William Hare

And...

There's an auld Scottish saying, here's how it goes -
- that the greed of a man may break more than his nose.

Ghost Tour

Barry Bensdorp

A baleful burst of rain swept across the cobblestone courtyard and the few pedestrians out on a cold Sunday night scrambled for cover. Colin wished he was one of them. Instead, he slouched with his hands in his pockets, watching on as his girlfriend excitedly spoke with a Ghost Tour guide. He had half an ear on the conversation and half an eye on the warming sight across the other side of the courtyard, where people were sitting and drinking inside a cosy bar. He turned back wistfully as his girlfriend nudged him and turned his attention to what the tour guide was saying.

“Normally I wouldn't, not just for two people and especially not on a night like this but if it's your last night in Edinburgh, well, I could do a shorter version of the walk that I promise will have you stone cold shaking in fear,” the guide announced in a deep and theatrical manner, his voice easily carrying over the fitful bursts of wind and rain. Colin's girlfriend gave a little jump and tugged on the sleeve of his rain jacket, “OK?” she asked as the last of the days quickly fading light illuminated her pretty freckled face.

"Yeah, s'pose," Colin replied, "How much?"

"Ten pound each for the tour and the frights are free," smiled the guide. He was a good head taller than both Colin and his girlfriend and his scraggly black beard was matched in untidiness by his battered black trench-coat. Colin pulled out his wallet and reluctantly handed over a twenty pound note. The guide quickly pocketed the money, took a step back and cleared his throat. "Lady, gentleman, before we start, take a look around this small courtyard, take a note of the name of the drinking establishment and take note of the two exits from the courtyard itself."

"It's called the Hanging Stone Inn," whispered Colin's girlfriend. Colin nodded, thinking twenty quid would have got him a few pints, a warm interior and not some lame ghost walk that had the added benefit of a damp Scottish drizzle running down the back of his neck. He followed the rapt gaze of his girlfriend towards the two exits, old blackish and grey stone arches before turning back to the tour guide who was speaking again.

"The Hanging Stone Inn, its history is one of blood, but none reputedly was ever spilt here. Long before it was a bar and a place of conviviality, it was a place of an entirely different type of spirit. Edinburgh was a very different place around the turn of the seventeenth century and at that time this was the house of Mr Thomas Melrose; confidant of the Lord Provost, Church Warder, Architect, Stone Mason, father of twelve and overseer to over three hundred deaths. Some by drowning, some by sword, some by rope and most with a heavy stone hung around their necks," he said in a deliberate tone as he shifted his gaze between that of Colin and his girlfriend. Colin smiled back, wondering how long a shortened tour was going to take and whether or not the pub would still be open by the time they got back.

"The guilty were paraded through the northern arch, made to stand and await judgement. In summer it could get to over ninety degrees Fahrenheit and the men, women and sometimes, little children," he said, pausing for emphasis. "Little children were left to stand, to wait. No water, no food, no footwear. For up to six hours they stood and waited for Mr Melrose. Some passed out, many lost control of their bladders.

The hardy ones stood silent and strong, but all waited for the same verdict, guilty and guilty of what? In winter it was worse, snow would cover the courtyard and here they would stand, wet, hungry and freezing. The chilblains on their feet growing ever blacker, hypothermia setting in, some passed out, and some died on the cold stone. They were the lucky ones. Some went delirious and others waited silent and strong for their verdict. That same verdict, guilty."

"Guilty of what?" asked Colin's girlfriend, her voice a squeaky whisper.

"Heresy dear girl; heresy against the church and heresy against the city. It was demanded by Melrose, my way or the highway. For the guilty, the highway led from the northern arch, through the square, through the southern arch and down into the burial grounds. No court of appeal, no recourse to justice and no mercy from church or state. In this city, in this dark, unsettled time, the church and state was Thomas Melrose and Thomas Melrose was not a lenient man," the guide answered and turned to point at the southern arch. "Let us walk down to the arch, undercover from the rain and continue the story." So saying, he clapped his hands and quickly strode through the courtyard towards the southern arch.

"Heresy dear girl," mimicked Colin in a whisper to his girlfriend and they both giggled and hurried off after the guide. The guide stopped at the base of the arch and knelt, beckoning the two tourists to do the same.

“Tell me, what you can see?” he asked his voice urgent and excited.

Colin looked down at the cobblestones. Underneath the arch the street was dry and in the dying twilight Colin remarked that all he could see were cobblestones.

“Look closer, there is a difference,” the guide prompted dramatically. Colin looked down again, “Um, they're dry?” he hazarded.

“No,” his girlfriend squealed, “they have a hint of red to them.”

“Blood,” shouted the tour guide and both Colin and his girlfriend leapt to their feet.

“Bloody hell,” Colin exclaimed.

“Exactly young man, bloody hell and the stains remain to this day, seeped into the stone never to be washed away, never to be forgotten, never to be forgiven.”

Colin's girlfriend shrunk into his side, grabbing him around his waist. The tour guide drew out a rusty length of chain and theatrically pulled it along the stones. “Dragged, bleeding and cursing. Beneath the arch they all came, in chains, in ropes, in incoherent screams and in despair.

Quickly, this way," he shouted and jogged toward the end of the small arched tunnel. He stood silhouetted by the far off street light, his elongated profile, ominous and black. He pointed at the stone arched ceiling. "Look," he cried with urgency.

Colin and his girlfriend hurried over and locked their eyes to where the tour guide was gesturing. "Look, it's opened," he exalted.

Colin thought he saw an image of a gaping mouth etched into the stone. Thin stone lips with oversized, sharp stone teeth and heard the tour guide exhale and coldly whisper, "The drinker, still it thirsts, still it waits."

"The drinker, what's the drinker?" asked Colin's girlfriend timidly, her eyes fixated on the mouth. She circled slowly, gazing at it from every angle.

"OK, who is the drinker?" Colin said on queue.

"Legend has it that when Melrose died some two hundred and eighty years ago, he was given a good Christian burial. Three days after, the mouth appeared - coincidence? Is it Melrose? Perhaps a carving as a form of remembrance from one of his stone mason colleagues, perhaps something even more sinister?" the tour guide pronounced.

"Like what?" Colin asked, on queue again.

"We now know from scraps of letters and journals, that good Thomas Melrose, family man, Church Warder, Mayor and let's not forget, mass murderer was tithing to an altogether darker force than that of the church, but let's not get ahead of ourselves in our tale," the guide answered, swinging his black coat about himself and walking from under the arch into the darkening night.

"Wait on," Colin shouted, "so who is the drinker?"

"Follow me," the guide shouted back, skipping along the dark cobbled lane.

Colin paused, but at the insistent tug of his girlfriend, he hurried after the guide.

The guide had stopped under a single lamppost. He stood at a Y intersection where the lane split into two. The weak fluorescent light gave him an unnaturally pale and fevered visage. He waited for his two tourists to catch up and swept his arms in a wide arc. "The high road," he said pointing to his left, "and the low road," similarly pointing to his right.

"Which one did for the victims and which one did for Melrose?" he asked.

"The low road did for them both," exclaimed Colin's

girlfriend.

"Well, well. We have a ghost hunter in our midst," chortled the guide.

"No, it's just that there are more of those red stones and they're only on the downside. There don't seem to be any leading up."

"And that is why we too will take the low road, but first a cautionary word before we reach our final resting point. Melrose it has to be said, though a family man and a respected man, was most definitely a madman and those he sentenced to death, died horrifically. In fear, alone, gibbering and pleading. Men, women and children, guilty of little more than being in the wrong place and in the wrong time and here is the caution. As I said earlier, it is believed that Melrose was tithing to darker forces, to things beyond the human realm. Fearful realms, dark realms, entities and places that should not be entreated with, cannot safely be entreated with. Entities of some power, entities that do not diminish and still hunger."

Colin found himself wrapping a protective arm around his girlfriend. For the first time that night, even he admitted to feeling a first pang of unease.

"It is this collection of fear, this accumulation of

terrible deeds, this construct of evil by so many deaths that has caused these phenomena to exist, and it is our fear and our anxiety that continues to feed it. This is why only our tour goes down in the dark of night, the others steer well clear, but I caution you again, do you really want to see this? If not, turn away now. "

He paused, brushed his damp black hair from his face and said in a most solemn and serious tone, "Shall we go on?"

Colin and his girlfriend looked at each other in the settling darkness underneath the street light. They nodded to the tour guide to continue.

"At the bottom of the lane is where the old burial ground was. Now long covered over, built upon over the centuries. Market stalls replaced with single story shops built of stone, a baker, a bank, lawyers' offices and then demolished. Now it is a non-descript engineering firm with a second story car park. All that remains from three hundred years ago is one stretch of corner wall and there we go for the final part of our tour. There Melrose or some other force, some other evil awaits."

"And we're going there because?" Colin asked trying to sound light-hearted.

“To see the ghosts,” wailed the tour guide dramatically as he pulled out a small pen torch and shone it up to his face. Colin's girlfriend clapped her hands and let out a squeal. “Wow, a real ghost tour. Will we really see ghosts?”

“Guaranteed,” exclaimed the tour guide.

“What, like bit part actors sneaking up from behind us, wailing and giving us a good scare?” Colin stated with somewhat false bravado.

“Who knows what waits in the dark?” the guide said shining his torch and proceeding down the dark low lane. Colin followed; keeping his eye's fixed to the torch light. The small beam gave scant illumination and with the sun set, the broody, cloudy sky was now a fitful mass of ever darkening hues. An occasional gust and burst of drizzle swept up the winding lane. Colin hunched forward trying to keep in the warmth from his down jacket and squeezed the hand of his girlfriend. “You believe all this?” he whispered to her.

“I don't know, but he's very good. I've got goose bumps all over and not from the cold.”

The ghost tour guide had come to a stop where the lane levelled out. “The buildings we walked past, many of them are still the original ones from three centuries ago. New windows, doors and restored inside, but the outer stone work has been witness to the passing by of bleeding feet, the cries of the gaunt and injured, the wails of the old and innocent. Melrose it is reported never actually came down to see the final executions, the blood being shed, the burials, and the final entombment of the guilty."

He shone his torch upon the sign of the engineering shop, "McMeechan Motors" it read and then he moved the torchlight to a small alleyway between the shop and a ten foot stone wall, leaving the small beam of light to rest on a small brass plaque. "Here it is, consigned to history by a small brass memorial and a non-descript entry in local guide-books, but kept alive in the hearts and minds of ghost hunters such as yourselves by yours truly," and he gave a small bow.

Colin walked up to the plaque, the inscription simply read; "The Hanging Stone wall."

"The same name as the pub from the courtyard," he exclaimed, looking over to the guide.

"Indeed, this wall was made from the stones that were hung around the victims necks. Built by the supposed guilty to wall in the ground where they would spend their eternal rest. Many want the story to remain buried, just like the hundreds of bodies below us. Rotted away, ashes to ashes, dust to dust, but we remember. Look, there is proof in the wall itself."

He turned into the alleyway and shone his torch to a spot in the lower corner where the wall met the side of the engineering workshop. The old stone wall was a collection of misshapen dark grey and black stone, damp with lichen. Near the base a puddle had formed from the day's rain, unable to drain away. The tour guide beckoned Colin and his girlfriend closer, a purposeful look on his thin bearded face.

"It's a red hand-print," Colin's girlfriend whispered.

"Aye, and look further up," exhorted the guide. They followed the light of the torch up a few feet and both Colin and his girlfriend jumped back. Imprinted in the stone was the semblance of a grisly face, caught in mid scream. There was a small thread of reddish colouring as if they were drops of blood dripping from its forehead.

"Three hundred years of suffering. Trapped in the earth, trapped in stone, not guilty, but sentence passed. They do not rest and their suffering continues. This is where the wicked lie," and so saying he waved his torch like a sword, criss-crossing the alley, strobe lighting around Colin and his girlfriend, light, dark, yellow, black and he laughed as he did.

"Make him stop Colin, he's scaring me," wailed the girl and as she did the guide switched the torch off.

They were plunged into darkness, there was no moon or starlight that could break through the thick cover of cloud and no street light radiated into the alleyway. Colin's girlfriend shrieked and backed against the wall. Suddenly the torchlight flicked on, the tour guide stood blocking the front of the alley, smiling. "Scared, just a little?"

"Bloody hell that was a mean trick," Colin shouted.

"Trick, no trick..... turn around..... look at the wall."

Colin turned following the beam of the torch. Another section of the wall was lit by the thin shaft of light. Another hand, another deformed face. This face looked as if it was pushing itself out of the wall, were they real rivulets of blood dripping from its forehead and sharpened teeth in a distorted mouth and below, was that a hand clutching at his girlfriend?

The tour guide moved forward, pushing Colin nearer to the wall. "Feed the fear," he hissed.

Colin tried to hold his ground and choked back his fear.

He swung wildly, flailing with his hands and connected with the tour guide's arm. He made a hurried grab for the torch, but unbalanced they both fell towards the wall. “No,” cried the tour guide as the small pen torch slipped from his grasp. The torch hit the ground and the tiny bulb popped. There was a brief, quiet noise of breaking glass as the alley was plunged into darkness, but not into silence. A terrible grating of shifting stone, three stifled screams and then deathly quiet as the drinker quenched its thirst.

Beyond These walls

Sarah Guppy

Luis Castanas works steadily at the wallpaper with a scraper. Slowly, the paper is coming off but he has to keep on applying a damp cloth to the walls to moisten and loosen the paper first. It is a laborious process, but already one whole wall opposite has been done. He was born in Spain but has been living in Edinburgh for the last few months. He has an apartment in the basement of a tall elegant Georgian house in North Castle Street. He loved these elegant houses; he could look up from his windows through the railings and see people's feet and legs walking by on the pavement above. He can make a stink with his Spanish cooking, tortilla and garlic and nobody would complain; he is tucked away out of sight with a separate, hidden front door. The wallpaper looks like it might be 1970s with swirling big garish flowers in clashing colours.

He has been given permission to strip the paper by the flat's owner – a wealthy corporate lawyer who he had met and got talking to on the plane. Alistair Macintyre, a balding and middle aged product of Fettes College, had taken a liking to the Spanish man in his thirties. He saw ambition and a fighting spirit. Alistair lives hectically in the rest of the enormous house above and seems to be either engaging in frantic social networking or flying off abroad. They had been sitting next to each other on the plane and Luis had mentioned that as a child he had seen 'Kidnapped' dramatised in to a series on TV and translated in to Spanish. The red coats, the Highlands and the brave man called David captivated him as a small boy. It was supposed to be a holiday but Alistair had offered him the basement flat to stay in for a year at reduced rent.

The idea is to paint the bedroom and hall when all this paper had come off. Over a year ago Alistair had bought some white paint with a hint of lemon yellow and it had just been gathering dust in the front room all this time. Luis has offered to paint the flat and put some shelves in the bedroom – explaining that he is a carpenter and decorator by trade. Stopping to sip at some espresso coffee, he thinks again of the pretty young waitress he had chatted to in the small café in Register Place to the left of Register House which imposed its grand, official façade on to Princes Street. He had been there quite a lot on his days off and had gathered that her name was Shona. Sometimes he'd just order a coffee, at other times maybe a ham sandwich or something hot. She had very blonde hair with freckles which had been another boyish dream of his.

He had caught her looking at him shyly and had wondered when he should make a move and ask her out.

Although his English was not great and he struggled with letters like ‘th’ it was still coherent enough. Alistair had helped him get some work doing joinery and putting up shelves and skirting in other properties – this had been cash in hand. His main part time job though was in the Scott Monument where he worked as a temporary guide and ticket seller to cope with the extra influx of tourists during the summer. He had climbed all 287 steps and had seen views from the very top. He finishes his coffee and looks at his watch: only half past eleven. He could go to the café later and maybe ask her then. After a cool shower he could put on his smart yellow shirt which brought out his olive skin.

Scruffy looking pigeons often land on the monument ledges which Luis had to clear off. Wire mesh has been put over some of the stone carvings as a way of preventing them from nesting in the nooks and crannies. Usually the busiest times are between noon and two o’clock but he had to control total visitor numbers that went up there at any time. The building, though strong, has its limits and people needed to be able to climb up and down without congestion. Most tourists were well behaved but a few treated him with pity. Some of the children stared at him in his uniform asking their parents what the man was doing shooing the birds away. When he first got the job he had enjoyed exploring the monument, admiring the way animals and detail were to be found in every available space. There was a green, mossy feel and look to the stones.

It had been during one unusually quiet afternoon that he first saw what he thought was a cloaked figure of someone on the security TV screen in the little ticket office by the entrance door. He blinked and the figure had disappeared and yet he had sold no tickets in the last hour. To his knowledge, nobody was on the monument at all. It was strange. He had forgotten about it and had not mentioned it to his colleagues for fear of being laughed at. Then there had been the other time, at closing time, when he was just quickly climbing down the steps after checking nobody was still up there – it happened quickly - but he was sure he could hear someone else coming down the steps above him. The two occurrences had happened quite soon after he had started to strip the wallpaper away at the flat he reflects.

Alistair is a good landlord, coming downstairs to check on him once a month and collect the rent. He had taken Luis out to supper a couple of times in the New Town. "I'm not sure how many layers of wall paper there are in there – could be older stuff under the more modern stuff. But it all has to come off please. People like the modern slick distressed light look – there's no market for musty paper."

Luis had asked what 'distressed' meant. "Stylishly worn painted walls, basically," Alistair had laughingly replied, pouring more wine. Alistair knows Luis is restless for love and has agreed that he can use his second home, a flat in Portobello - as long as he is discrete and gives him notice. Luis is proving to be a damn good decorator after all, a real find

The café is pretty busy as it's lunch time but Luis still manages to catch Shona's eye. Nearby construction work has brought in dust covered builders and scaffolders eager for quick hot grub and they jostle and joke with each other in the take away queue. He has grabbed a small table by the front window and waits for his chance. She comes round in an apron taking orders on a small pad. Two huge hoop earrings dangle from her ears.

“You want to meet later for a drink or a coffee?” he asks after he orders. Pause. She looks uncertain.

“We don’t have to be late or anything. Just one drink if you like” he further offers.

He suggests the Hilton hotel bar as it’s easy to find in Princes Street. Back at the flat, Luis wets the walls again and applies the scraper. Decent sized scrolls of moist paper curl and fall away to the floor. Underneath the flowery 1970s looking stuff is a much more sober print with ornate but ordered flowers. And working on in to the early evening, he discovers a layer of varnish covering yet another final layer of paper with stripes and tiny wreaths of fruit. Alistair had warned him that he may come across varnish as folk used to “protect their assets” as wallpaper was expensive then, he said. For Luis, this is yet another sign of British eccentricity. This last layer of wallpaper is only on one wall in the bedroom so sometime in the past it had been scraped off from the other walls very much as Luis is doing now. Who were these other silent scrapers and workers who decorated this house Luis wonders, as he tackles the ancient varnish. There is a faint smell as the stuff is removed. Were they hired immigrants. What secrets did this wallpaper hide, what conversations witnessed. He feels vaguely as if he committing some terrible act of sacrilege destroying these relics and the past that the British seem so peculiarly attached to.

At seven he meets her in the bar and they sit on big crackly black leather sofas trying to avert their eyes from the huge television screen broadcasting a live rock gig from a park somewhere. A few other punters stare at the screen and a group of American women come in to the bar then ordering whisky. Earlier, he had scrubbed his tongue and his teeth with toothpaste and he can taste the mint. She is wearing shimmery lipstick and high shoes with a floaty silky dress which also shimmers when she moves. She almost looks like a mirage she is shimmering so much and yet Luis knows she is real – so real he wanted to squeeze and lick her all over.

They talk about Scotland and what she wants to do in the future. She mentions that she's doing a hairdressing course at college in the evenings – so sometimes she goes to college straight after work. Had she ever been to Spain, he asks nervously after getting a second round of drinks. She giggles a no but mentions that she'd like to go one day – giving him a significant glance before downing the tequila. Play it by ear. Later, he suggests a walk and they stroll along Princes Street gardens in the July evening.

People sprawl out on the lawns drinking and picnicking in the warmth and light. They walk past the monument and glancing up, he sees a man in a cloak walking about on the second platform. Not again. But then they see the cameras and bright lights; the clapper board boy and other actors in costume who saunter around with the man on the monument. He takes her hand in his and whispers what he has in mind.

In a mist they get the 26 bus down to Portobello. He lets them in to Alistair's flat which over looks the sea and tells her she is a Scottish Venus emerging from the waves. The flat has large bay windows with fine views. He wakes in the early hours, glancing back down at her in the bed. She snores slightly. He stares out at the calm flat sea. In Spain the sea always looks blue or green but over here it was so many shades which changed almost every other minute. A bit like Scottish women's eyes that seem so gentle. And that was what he noticed about Shona the first time he saw her; the fact that her eyes seem to change colour like the sea. Falling asleep, he dreams he sees Shona in some costume waving to him from the monument. He is standing on nearby grass looking up at her not understanding what she is shouting down to him. He gestures that she should come down to talk to him but she teasingly shakes her head. It is then that he notices her dress which has the same stripes and small wreaths of fruit that he had seen on the ancient wallpaper he had scraped away in the flat. Shona looks frightened then as she hears someone coming up the steps. He thinks he glimpses a flash of cloak but then she screams and Luis cannot see anything any more.

Luis finishes the painting finally. The varnish was a bastard to remove but finally all walls in the bedroom and hall gleam with fresh paint. He is meeting Shona later, on the monument, as she says that she's not been up it despite growing up in Edinburgh. Will he hold her hand, she asks. She is a bit frightened of heights so she may have to stop at the first platform. Since that first date in the Hilton bar and later in Portobello, things have gone from strength to strength. Alistair has provided more work through his vast social network but still Luis wants to take Shona back to Almeira to meet his parents. It is a warm early September. He enjoys the mellow air. He walks up to the monument staring at it for a moment. It is a slightly forbidding looking structure – capable of hiding shadows. He glances up then suddenly to see Shona waving and shouting at him from the first platform. He cannot catch what she is saying, so she leans dangerously over a carved ledge. She almost slips in a heart churning moment and screams out for help.

At the flat in North Castle Street, Luis tends to the bruise on Shona's leg. It is an alarming blue purple colour but the cold flannel seems to sooth it. Shona appears subdued, perhaps slightly in awe of the sheer size and grandeur of the place. Alistair hears them coming in through the separate basement door and puts his head round the bedroom door to inspect the work. One can access the basement via the discreet door in the street as well as from the house above.

"Season of mellow fruitfulness, eh? "Good job, Luis. Knew you could do it. Had a hellish flight back from Hamburg on a real pig of a case. But this has cheered me up. Looks like there will be other work for you too as I have been talking you up like mad you know. You two care to join me for some wine upstairs?" Alistair smiles kindly at Shona who seems recovered. Upstairs, they sit and drink red wine in antique chairs as mellow evening sunlight pours in through sash windows.

"Hey guess what, Luis. Found out from Auntie in London that Sir Walter Scott stayed here briefly at one point to help with royal visit preparations. I'll have to think about a plaque of some sort. Will boost the value of the property no end of course. Funny that, eh?"

Luis shudders then but does not know why. Later, he sees Shona off in the street, kissing her tenderly and assuring her he will text her. He has recently acquired a mobile which seems to ring a lot now about decorating work.

He lets himself back in to the basement flat as darkness begins to descend. Switching on the bedroom light, he looks again at the walls. He is confused to see a patch of bedroom wall which he must have somehow missed – though he doesn't know how. Just visible through the paint, like a ghostly reminder of something, is the stripy wallpaper with the small wreaths of fruit.

Edinburgh Rock

Iddo Oberski

"Built on rock," they keep reminding me.
This town of great grey blocks,
sleepy in between the hills and river,
curving crescents, layered streets,
old tenements peering north
towards the new town (and the Forth).

A tentative capital,
"It's built on rock" they say,
as if it was a good excuse
for keeping me at arm's length still.
Can you ever judge a person
by the city of their birth?

To judge itself requires rock,
a strong foundation, not of course
of Earth, but reason and of heart.
"Of heart?" they ask "what right have you?"
and so it goes that I keep wandering
and wondering how can it be?

That with all its might and mystery
a city stands, not lies, upright between
the rolling hills and sea.
“It’s built on rock,” again they speak.
So it’s difficult to settle
if you’re a stranger in this place?

Expect a visitor’s welcome,
but do not stay, please do not stay,
the city begs as foreigners take root,
with too much difficulty.
“It’s built on rock” remember?
You need persistent roots

to finally embrace the rock
with penetrating tentacles,
through crevices and cracks.
Then yes then the city finally sighs and
lets you breathe its humid air.
For underneath this rocky place

there is perhaps invisible,
a provisional welcome, even a love
of difference and of strange.
A strangeness now come home
yet silently separated still
from something I cannot fathom.

Secret Edinburgh, built on rock.

A Sign From Heaven

Martin Arthur Paul Wilson

The details begin to change in my head. I think I can remember, but I've told the story many times now. Fact and fiction begin to intermingle as I decide on which elements would improve the telling, and which can go unmentioned. For instance now I begin to wonder whether it was the first exam, or the second. I am not sure, but I think it was the first. And of course, I can't check the details with anyone else.

It was late spring, early summer, one of those brilliant clear days that seems to happen in Edinburgh but not in Glasgow, where I could briefly believe that summer happened in Scotland. My sleeping cycle has never been much good, but I awoke early on that day, aware of the crisp, warm light sliding through our living room window. I found myself sitting in the sun soaked sofa, talking to Robbie.

"I suppose we've got to go," I said.

He nodded, his face dark despite the weather. I can't imagine mine looked better, even sitting opposite the window.

"What about Steven?" I asked.

Robbie shook his head.

"He's not coming."

"You phoned him?"

"We spoke last night."

I frowned.

"Maybe we should, I don't know, go round to his place and wake him up or something?" I said, "It's important."

Robbie shrugged.

"You know what he's like."

I sighed and nodded.

Of the three of us, Steven alone had not handed in his dissertation. Even to this day I hold myself to that low standard 'I did better than Steven'. Not much of a consolation in the end.

"Did you study?" I asked.

"A little. You?"

He gave me a look I didn't much like, the kind that said '*I know you haven't done a bit and there's no good hiding it.*' We had lived together for two years by this point, so he knew my habits pretty well.

"I put the books near my bed while I was asleep," I

said, “So, um, maybe the words would sort of sink in, like, while I was sleeping?”

Robbie grinned.

“Yeah,” he said, “Maybe.”

I swallowed, trying to ignore the feeling in my stomach, like it might burrow out of my body and run away to escape the shame.

Somehow, the prospect of failing the exam didn’t worry me as much as the idea of turning up and seeing the rest of the class hanging out outside the hall, with their books and their notes, revising away, but still ready to say, “Hey guys, where the hell have you been? We haven’t seen you in class for months.” Worse still, the lecturers might be there. I pictured the head of the department; a man who looked like a fifty year old Fonzie, with slick black hair and a wont to wear a leather jacket, yet with iron hidden behind his grin. I could see him asking what happened to the essays we were supposed to hand in earlier in the year. Were there four? Or five? I don’t think I could remember, even then.

I slipped into my shoes and jacket, stopping by my room briefly, debating whether or not it was worth picking up my shabby semblance of notes. I decided against it;

there was no point in embarrassing myself any further by showing them off. I checked my pockets for the usual paraphernalia of exams: my student card, to be placed face up on my desk, my phone, to be set to silent and dumped half way across the hall in case I had contrived some way to telepathically send and receive texts using a phone locked in my pocket.

I paused.

"Robbie," I asked, "Have you got a spare pen?"

My last pen had broken or run out months ago. Poking around the flat and Edinburgh, using my PC or hanging out, I hadn't needed a replacement. It was only now that I realised I didn't have one.

"Why?" he asked, "Don't you?"

"No."

"Uhhh... I was going to ask you for one."

"You don't have one either?" I asked.

"No."

"Damn."

"Oh well," he said, shrugging, "We'll just have to buy some on the way."

I nodded.

Our route took us through one of the main arteries of Edinburgh, a street I had named "Buystuff Road" in the naiveté of first year when "Nicolson Street" sounded confusing and alien when it was crowded together with half a dozen others.

The flat itself was excellently situated, although I maintain that this was our problem all along. In first year, Robbie had commuted to class from Glasgow. He was never late, unless the bus broke down. In second year we moved into a friend's flat, with only a walk across the Meadows to reach class. Our attendance got a lot worse; class was closer, close enough that we might leave it until, oh, say five minutes beforehand to leave. Maybe even on the hour, there's no harm in being five minutes late...

Our final flat was so close we could have virtually rolled out of bed and into class. And yet our attendance was worse in fourth year than ever before.

We slipped down the stairs and into the perfect clarity of that early summer weather. The city really was beautiful then, the only clouds in the sky wispy and cream-white, the dingy grey buildings turned brilliant pearl by the sun.

Tesco was less than five minutes walk from the flat, as close as class, although we managed to go to Tesco just about every day. I don't think we'd ever bought stationary before, though. It took ten minutes just to find the right aisle.

"Do you see any pens?" Robbie asked.

"No," I said, frowning, "It's all rules and binders and crap."

"C'mon, they *must* have pens."

"Aye, right, they will, they're just, I dunno, hidden. Maybe it's another part of Tesco's inscruitable marketing policy to try and convince us to buy more buns or something," I said.

"Wait, here we go," he said.

"Got 'em?"

"Nnno. They used to be here," he said, fingering the tag on the shelf, "Out of stock."

I bit my lip.

"I suppose we could use pencils. Wouldn't really be proper but-"

"Nope," he said, "All out too."

"Damn. I suppose there must be a run on, what with exams and everything?"

"Mmm."

"Oh well," I said, "There's always Scot-Mid."

He nodded.

Scot-Mid was directly opposite Tesco. It took less than a minute to figure out that they didn't stock any pens.

Robbie summed up the situation succinctly once we were back on the street;

"Bugger."

"We've got loads of time," I said. We may have missed the deadlines for many major essays, projects and pieces of coursework, but by God, we had made sure to leave for the exam over an hour in advance.

"Maybe we can get them somewhere further up?" I said, "There's that stationary shop along the way."

Robbie nodded. It'd be a bit out of the way, but we couldn't exactly sit the exam without pens, now, could we?

"I can't believe it," he said.

"I don't understand. It's a stationary shop."

The girl at the counter looked at us wistfully and shook her head.

"It's really more of a printing shop," she said.

"This is serious," Robbie said, turning to me, "We *need*

some pens."

"Right," I said, "Right. Only, wait, hold on. What if it's a sign?"

"... a sign?"

"Yeah. A sign *from the Gods*."

Robbie looked at me.

We were both self confessed atheists or agnostics. My only major dalliance with religion was a deep affection for Greek and Norse Gods.

"They're trying to tell us something," I said, "Maybe if we cannot find any pens then we are not supposed to go to the exam?"

"... That's stupid," he said, although he was smiling.

"It's a sign," I said, nodding to myself.

"Look, this is the heart of studentland," he said, gesturing to the broad area surrounding the University, "You can't have five vegan restaurants within walking distance of each other without having any pens for sale."

I nodded.

"You're right," I said.

"Come on," he said, "We'll check the next place-there's plenty."

There were plenty of shops, but apparently not plenty of pens. We checked the little electronics shops and the news agents up and down 'Buystuff Road' but none of them seemed big on writing implements. I noted each one.

"If there's nothing in the next shop," I said, "It must be a sign."

Robbie didn't say anything then, I was clearly on the verge of not only proving the existence of God, but that it was divine will that we not sit our exam. What could he say in the face of that?

Tesco Metro was last on the list- or was it Tesco Express? A second Tesco, not far from the first. Tesco were keen on opening more shops then, I think since they've developed Tesco Micro or something, a Tescos so small that it fits in your pocket. This one was smaller than the first, but hardly more likely to stock what we needed. We popped in, sweeping up and down the aisles in a desultory search for our missing stationary.

Moments later we were standing dead still in front of a crowded stationary stand at the edge of the shop.

Dangling from hooks were more than a dozen bright blue plastic pens, gleaming in the harsh artificial light of the shop.

I looked at Robbie.

He looked at me.

"Do you see any pens?" he asked.

I turned back, looking at them, row upon row of pens sitting there, trying to shatter my newfound religion.

I turned back to Robbie.

"I see no pens," I said.

Robbie nodded, grimly.

"It's a sign," he said, "from the gods."

We spent the day strolling around parts of Edinburgh we had never seen before. We saw the dubious artwork that is the Scottish Parliament, and watched the shadows of clouds play upon Arthur's Seat. Then we fell into a discussion about whether or not Arthurian legend was Welsh. Eventually, long after the exam was over, we went back to the flat.

We went to some of the exams in the end. I think I spent most of the language exam utterly bamboozled, waiting for someone else to leave first so that I didn't have be the first one out. Steven didn't sit a single one, but, well, you know what he's like.

We failed, of course. I got a B on my dissertation, I was

quite proud of that, but we failed just about every exam we sat, to say nothing of the three or four we skipped. In Winter we graduated, awarded a Bachelor of Arts in Humanities and Social Sciences.

I tell people 'I studied Japanese for four years, and got a degree,' now, carefully neglecting to mention that the degree wasn't in Japanese.

***

Robbie died just before Christmas last year, knocked down by a car.

I told people the story afterwards; friends, his family. I had been embarrassed before, shameful. But suddenly after that it didn't seem so bad any more. We had laughed that day, and there had been a strange, fragile spirit of excitement in the air. I barely remember the subsequent failed exams, but the day of no pens lingers on.

The Pilrig Pudding

Barry Bensdorp

The elderly Guesthouse keeper waited patiently as her only guest finished the last morsels of food on the plate. Her expression was dignified and matched the décor of the dining room. The dark Scots pine panelling rose halfway up the wall to a simple blue and white X patterned wall paper. There were several fading prints on the far wall, the construction of the Forth rail bridge, the Clyde shipyards and strangely, a North Sea Oil rig. There were two walnut display cabinets with carefully placed bric-a-brac. There were heather painted cups, saucers, thimbles, a few decorative spoons emblazoned with the Edinburgh Coat of Arms and several daggers with thistle shaped handles. To one side of the cabinets and at odds with the rest of the room, mounted on the wall were three lion's or more precisely three tatty shrunken lion heads.

Her guest finished the last forkful of food and looked around appreciatively, his eyes coming to rest on the three lions. "Three lions, I'm sure they have an interesting history," he remarked.

"Ach no, those old things, truly stuffed," Mrs Balfour,

the proprietor of the house replied. Mrs Balfour kept a tidy house, everything in its place and everyone in their place and as in the case of her one current guest, that place was at her dining room table. She watched on as he carefully placed his fork and knife on to his empty plate and shuffled back in his seat.

"Splendid meal Mrs Balfour, absolutely splendid. A meal that rivals the magnificence of this city," proclaimed the well-dressed man, dabbing his lips with a well pressed napkin. His precise and clipped tones were distilled from the very essence of public schooling. Mrs Balfour beamed, the smile adding even more wrinkles to her elderly face. "Thank you Mr W, I've always been proud of my table here at the guesthouse. Did you have any trouble locating the Guesthouse here in Pilrig? After all, you've travelled some way to be with us."

"Not that great a distance, London is only seven hours by car."

"Seven hours but an entirely different country, that's far in my book. In seven hours you could be in all sorts of foreign places but here you are, safe and sound. Was it a tiring drive?" she asked politely.

"Oh no, the chauffeur is an excellent driver," Mr W

replied.

"Will he be joining us at all? I've only catered for one."

"No, no, definitely not. Bit of family history there, don't like to talk about it, them, chauffeurs, I hope you understand. Enough of that though, splendid meal, splendid."

"I try my best."

"And you succeed. Your fine meal and your fine house is a welcome change to some of the mishmash that I usually have to deal with. One can only take so much Victorian, Georgian and Edwardian. One must admit that your genteel interior is a balm."

Mrs Balfour beamed again as she collected up the dishes and cutlery. "Could I tempt you with some pudding, coffee and perhaps a wee dram?"

"If your dessert is anywhere near the standard of your main, then I would be a fool to say no and a wee drop of single malt would be a capital idea, excuse the pun."

Mr W brushed an errant grey hair from his suit and watched it waft to the plush dark green tweed carpet. He stared absently out of the north facing bay window as the elderly Housekeeper cleared the table. The late setting sun created a dimpling diamond effect across the Firth. It was a rare feeling and an especial occasion to feel this relaxed.

"Pilrig, a peculiar name," he remarked absently.

"The tower at the end of the field, though now it's mostly tenements and buildings for the modern age. History seems to be a thing of the past," Mrs Balfour replied in passing as she made her way back to the kitchen.

Some minutes passed and Mrs Balfour returned to the dining room bearing a tray which she carefully placed on the white linen topped table. She took the cup and saucer and placed it in front of her one and only guest. "Coffee, I took the liberty, white and weak."

"A fine cook and a good judge of character," smiled Mr W taking a small sip and nodded his liking of the coffee. His gaze followed Mrs Balfour as she picked up a whisky tumbler and a bottle of whisky from the tray. "Glenkinchie, a local distillery only several miles to the east. I try and source all of my produce from local sources. Lothian lamb, Midlothian mint, carrots from Corstophine…."

"And Jersey Royals I hope," interrupted Mr W.

Mrs Balfour looked aghast, "Oh no, none of that foreign muck on my plates," she said as she sloshed a finger of the single malt into the glass. Her accent slipping as she pushed the glass towards her guest. "Now git tha' doon thee," and turning on her heel she stomped out, leaving her bewildered guest gaping like a fish.

He took another sip of the whisky and let the gentle malt taste suffuse his mouth. Relaxing again, he took another sip and admired the parochialism of the room, the warmth and straight forwardness of the furnishings and the tell-tale signs of a comfortable life, well lived. Home was never like this he thought.

Several more minutes passed and the Housekeeper returned with a large wooden chopping board which she gently placed on the table. "Do you like the whisky?" she asked, her voice returned to its former polite and clipped tone.

"Very smooth. Some nutty barley, mild fruity tones and a hint of honey, very much to my liking."

"Nutty and fruity, I wouldn't have guessed. Well then, I'm sure that you'll like my pudding then," she remarked, leaving the dining room once more, only to return within the minute carrying a huge white enamel bowl with a chipped blue rim. She expertly turned the bowl upside down as steam billowed from the sides. "As my dear mother used to say; if the fid was gid, the pud would be better," said Mrs Balfour as she lifted the bowl, revealing a huge round, solid and steaming pudding. "Clootie dumpling, made from the freshest and finest local ingredients, currants, sugar, spice, treacle and most importantly, the flour of Scotland."

"Amen to that."

"Are you a religious man at all?" she asked, reaching behind her apron and pulling out a large blunt cleaver of greyish steel. She cleaved the dumpling in two. "There we are, one for the Protestants and one for the Catholics. Do you have a preference?"

"That's an awfully large dumpling," remarked Mr W, shaking his head at the size of the massive pudding. "I'm not sure if one could finish such a large piece."

"Well then, let's make it a bit easier to plate then," said Mrs Balfour. The cleaver come down again, halving the half's. "There we are, one for Scotland, one for England, one for Wales and the other for Ireland."

Mr W coughed and shifted uncomfortably in his chair.

"Well, yes, uh-hum, the United Cake of Britain, however daunted by the size of such a slice, I'm bound by my standing to the obligation of an attempt," he said somewhat weakly.

"Standing, well of standing I'm sure you are a prince among men so would that be ruling, upper, middle or working? Though for them that can't, should we even let them eat cake?" Mrs Balfour replied as she sectioned the dumpling with another four sharp blows.

"And then we'll have a piece for Rabbie, for the Clavie, St Andrew and the Wickerman." Chop, cleave, chop. "Candlemas and the Scoorie," Chop, chop.

Mr W pushed back from the table, running a hand though his thinning hair. His ruddy cheeks glowing from the whisky and shock of the constantly falling blade.

"And a parcel of pudding for the Gowk, for Baal at Beltane," the cleaver sliced again and again. "Save a slice for Lammas, for Marymas and the poor at Martinmas." The dumpling was now speckled across the board, across the table. Currants dotted the once pristine table cloth and the pungent aroma of the Clootie filled the room.

"A pudding for all, for Sowans Nicht, for the Yule, for Hogmanay, we'll eat this pudding yet, for the sake of auld lang syne," Mrs Balfour sang, cleaving the last pieces into small crumbled remnants. She turned to face her guest, cleaver in hand. Her apron and long black skirt were flecked with crumbs and her once tidy grey hair waved riotously around her face. A smile lit up her face and the wildness left her eyes. She carefully positioned the cleaver on the table and took a bowl and a spoon from the serving tray.

Mrs Balfour, the Head of her Household reached across the table and placed a bowl and spoon in front of the quivering Mr W. She primly walked to the dining room door, straightening her apron and her posture. Deliberately pausing she faced her guest, calmness and pride had returned and with a parting retort she left the room, "The dumpling is done and to your house do I devolve my final duties."

Room Service

Sarah Guppy

Robert McLair-Turner sits in the hotel room smoking a filter tip cigarette. It's a plush green and gold sofa he is sitting on in a discrete hotel room near to Shandwick Place. He's just returned from the all important meeting which happened that morning in the bank's HQ. He had agreed to add a number of investment bonds to his work portfolio. Overseas bond markets are his speciality. Rain spits on to the Edwardian room's windows – nevertheless he can still decipher the Scott Monument looming in the distance. He went up there once as a child when he'd been growing up in dank Gorgie. A product of a divorced Scottish father and English mother, he migrated South at the first available opportunity. He gently fingers the dog eared calling card he'd found in the metallic looking public pay-as-you-go toilets near the Square. To call or not to call that was always the question. But Dr. Behr in London thinks he's making good progress, he has had no lapses for over a year. It's a terrible kind of closed circuit in the mind that sets him off; he has to *dismiss the thoughts* as Dr. Behr advised. And Robert is now doing good, our Scottish man based in London.

Sucking on the cigarette thoughtfully, he rings reception for a light supper to be brought up.

"Would sir like any wine with that?" asks the young Australian girl.

Robert selects a medium table red, not too fruity. The girl tells him it will be fifteen minutes. A glance at the watch. Five thirty. The mobile sits enticingly by the calling card on the glass topped table. So easy. With an effort of will, Robert switches on the lap top. And stuff the general public frankly; the great unwashed just didn't understand the way international investment banking worked. He had to admit though that some of the amounts of capital flows involved were eye scorching. How many schools or missile defence mechanisms did this amount to? God knows. Still, it was people like him who brought money in to the country, the politicians knew it. We are the guys who call the shots ultimately he thinks. He examines slight changes in fund values. A knock on the door and a girl brings in Robert's food and wine on a tray. After eating he flicks on the wide screen TV but instantly becomes bored. He is due to fly back down South tomorrow morning. He is used to this fly-by-night life by now. Munich, NY, Basle, Tokyo - often at short notice. Always prepared though.

The West End and Shandwick Place hasn't changed that much he thinks, as Robert watches late suited office workers finishing up for the day and homeless people begging for money in tattered blankets. The last time he visited Edinburgh was two years ago when he attended his father's funeral. Mother is in a private care home in Corstorphine and Robert tries to visit her every six months. At least that is often the plan. It didn't actually happen that way and as an only child he wrestles regularly with guilt. On the balcony are little flower boxes stuffed with lobelia and pink and purple petunias which flutter in the rainy breeze. Minutes pass slowly. His whole existence is ruled and regulated by some clock, computer or camera somewhere. It's enough to drive a man to do strange wild things. Enough to tempt the mind to trick itself. And then conveniently to forget. And he surely knows the warning signs by now, the increased heart beat and momentary blurring of vision. The mobile taunts him silently and it is too late then. Some powerful magnetic force sucks him towards the glass topped table and he is dialling the number nervously before he can even think about it. It is always a thrill, this unknown. A rush. The loss of control then complete mastery. An oriental sounding woman answers to background music.

"You want to book boy?" the woman asks. "White, oriental, black?"

"White." Robert says.

"How old you want? Fourteen, fifteen, sixteen, older boy than that – maybe two boys you want?"

"Let's make it one boy at sixteen" Robert says. He gives the woman his suite number and the hotel's name.

"About forty minutes. Condom only" the woman says and hangs up abruptly. The woman had not asked about any optional side-lines, about things that could heighten intense pleasure.

***

He says his name is Murdo and that he is from Aberdeen. He had a terrible row with his violent junkie mother and had come down to Edinburgh where he had mates. He is wearing enormously baggy jeans that fall half way down his skinny arse and gold rings adorn practically every finger. Robert orders more wine to put Murdo at his ease.

"Smoke?" Robert offers the packet.

Murdo gratefully accepts a ciggie. They sit on the sofa

and Murdo mentions his dream about becoming a hairdresser.

"I've got mates in the business who could get me started," he explains.

After a while the small talk is over and Robert locks the suite's doors and they each take a hot shower and lie in the king sized bed. Robert runs his hand across the blond rough crew cut. Murdo's body is lithe and graceful in the room's twilight zone. For someone of such a tender age Murdo is very accomplished in the acts of love already. Robert marvels at the young flesh, acutely aware of his middle aged paunch and grey hairs.

"Will you come and do my hair in London?" teases Robert as patchouli oil is rubbed and massaged in to his chest. Murdo learnt fast and hadn't been daunted by handcuff or truncheon. Little optional extras that Robert couldn't resist carrying with him around the world. Sage Dr. Behr didn't need to know everything did he? After, they smoke more cigarettes and listen to the radio. Robert checks his lap top: already there are over twenty emails in his work mail box. He sits up in bed, tapping away whilst Murdo watches him carefully.

"What do you do for a job?" he asks. He is impressed

by what seems to him Robert's high speed high tech gadgets.

"I'm a corporate lawyer," Robert lies.

He knows he will never see the boy again, it's better this way. Anyway, he'd rather keep the two worlds he inhabits separate. Sex is just another market transaction. Nothing personal, no hard feelings. Best when it's anonymous and there's a slight element of risk – but that's it Christ knows, porn is the only growth industry he's aware of right now. Robert loves the transience of hotel rooms; everything was available at the touch of a button or at the end of a phone. No mess, no house work. Pay as you go in the here and now and no commitment required. Mail order food, male order fucks. You could be anybody in a hotel; you could assume a whole new you for a while. All part of the fun and games he muses. As long as you left no paper or electronic trails.

***

Robert eyes himself in the bathroom mirror. Still handsome, he considers. You old chancer, nobody could call *you* an old bore. He thought of his humble origins in Gorgie and then his scholarship to the fine grammar. He learnt some tricks there alright, about survival. Tricks from that old dog, the pure Maths master. He had searched hard for his pot of gold. Murdo had offered another round but Robert said he had to leave tomorrow, early. So he had paid him off with more fifty pound notes than he'd probably ever seen in his entire short life. "Good luck, hairdressing pal" he winked, shutting the door firmly. He didn't see it as exploiting the vulnerable; on the contrary, he was making sure the young lad earned something and didn't languish on benefits. His secretary, Linda, had e-mailed to let him know that Hans Bruner from Credit Suisse has called several times. Could he please call him as soon as – in case he didn't have the number here it is again. He appreciated that about Linda, her attention to detail. Linda is the only bank employee to know about this other side of his life; he has managed to engineer the double identities well. For Christ sake, he wasn't a paedo was he – he never went with lads under sixteen.

He showers again, washing away any trace of body odours. They even had hot showers at the Thames side office alongside state of the art restaurant, gym, pool, sauna and laundry services. In its way the building where he worked hid a multitude of sins. One could be cleansed, manicured and re-created afresh for the next day's trading; the next day's play. He wraps the condom in toilet tissue and puts it in the bin. As far as he can see there are no give away signs on the sheets. But then, horrors! He spies a few treacherous black pubic hairs and with clinical precision removes them. Leave no evidence, no trace. He still needs something more though. Some added side line. Murdo was good but a bonus is required just to reach the point of pure abstraction. To feel fully alive again and real. The line is duly re-created then on the glass top table, a pure white line of powder that magnifies and which will be absorbed by the bright white reasoning light in Robert's head. The needle scratches his arm as he plunges it in. He puts on a bathrobe after and washes his arm under the cold tap in the bathroom. Blessed oblivion. Twenty four hour nerves of steel need heightened blood flows after all. And both capital and blood must flow: it is in the very nature of things. The bodies, both corporate and human require it. It is the price. School had taught him *that* much. Redeeming darkness then sleep.

***

In the early morning Robert again checks the FTSE 100 companies and Wall Street for slight movements in bonds. What people didn't realise he thinks as he taps; is quite how *hard* bankers work. We never rest in the global economy. You cannot afford to. Yes, we do have place loyalty, a sense of commitment to place and people. We are not completely heartless. And my word is still my bond, though I cannae take responsibility for all other bond traders globally. Not everything is outsourced. Before the bank meeting he too had walked over the heart of Mid Lothian near St. Giles in the Royal Mile; he'd made a sincere wish the same as any other honest hard working hard playing tourist had. He wished the nasty recession would just go away. Could *he* help it as an individual if folk believed the narratives they were so often told and sold? These endlessly repeated narratives about utter necessities and inevitabilities. About sacrifices, rewards and opportunities and shared risk. About where we have come from, where we are now and where we are going. The story is told in Edinburgh, in Delhi, in Timbuktu. Hell, the story was told by Dickens. Only then *both* sex and tax were dodgy three letter words. As opposed to now Robert thinks cynically, casting his expert eye over an online article about tax evasion in the FT. And never mind the utter madness and powerlessness of hearing these endless cyclical stories despite living and working in the belly of the money machine itself. Did people think all bankers were bonkers about borrowing levels? He had watched TV coverage of the Wall Street protesters as well as the St. Paul's Cathedral protestors with his colleagues in various satellite offices.

Robert had seen the questions and the tents spread to Edinburgh too. And his colleagues were not completely unsympathetic. And this was the irony of the thing: people assumed that *they* the bankers were all insiders when in reality many often felt like outsiders. The other day he had freely given twenty pounds to a bedraggled looking busker by St. Giles –needing no prompt to give change. *That* kind of change was easy to bring about. And he regularly gives to charities which help the homeless down in London. When he first moved down South it had been touch and go for a while and he knew what it was like to have no permanent home. Throughout his recent expensive treatment, he has been ploughing through *Hard Times* right enough. Dr. Behr said reading is a good distraction, a good medicine. Soothes the all consuming fevers and cravings of the mind. Makes one temporarily forget dreams: dreams of perfection, of the impossibility of having it all, of inevitable impermanence even despite technology. For one has to have something to run on, apart from coffee and oil. And then there is of course the other matter he has to deal with. Of course Robert has not forgotten. This little visit to Old Reekie has been productive in more ways than one. He is a true dealer in every sense of the word after all. It, the small packet, is sitting safe in his brief case for now but he must devise a camouflage and arrange a drop off point for it to be collected tomorrow morning. He'll be back in London by then. It is light but eerily quiet outside; only a few cars can be heard. Princes Street is silent. The rain had obviously stopped at some point during the night; he hoped Murdo didn't get caught in it. Seemed like a nice young buck too. Robert is aware that he must try and find *somewhere* nearby to leave the packet. He is running out of time. But then, he has always been good at smuggling at the margins – whether on paper or on pavement. It is an art he does especially well. He climbs in to trousers and shirt then and walks around to the back of the hotel, hunting around. In a side street he sees a skip full of rubble and bricks. Perfect. Making a mental note of the street name, he returns to the hotel.

***

Munching on French toast later that morning Robert hits on the perfect ruse. Yes, the wit of it – the humour. Should have just about enough time before he catches the

100 bus to the airport. Nothing too obvious like a plastic bag or brown jiffy bag. Something domestic. He can engineer it if he works quickly. It will work fine. He can make the call after, when he is at the airport lounge. *You could call it his other side line,* he thought wryly. He calls down to reception saying the suite urgently needs a hoover, could someone please be sent up ASAP as he has an allergic reaction to dust. A few minutes later there is a gentle tapping on the door and a shy Asian lady comes in with duster and hoover. Robert waves his hand imperiously for her to start. Then, with the impeccable timing of an actor, he complains to the woman that the hoover cannot possibly work as the bag is way too full; it needs to be replaced, surely. The domestic looks alarmed and then confused. *God, where do they get these staff from* Robert thinks, as he breathes deeply. He squeezes the hoover bag and bulges out his cheeks for some visual dramatic effect, hoping she will see what he is saying. She starts laughing then and nods saying she will go and get a replacement bag. Perfect. He waits until she has left the room and then opens the suitcase and unfolds a cloth bag inside. The bagged powder inside is white and pure. Over a hundred grand's worth of top quality cocaine. Remarkable, really.

Deftly, he removes the hoover bag and puts the cloth bag and its precious contents in to it. He snaps the hoover bag back in to place. Smiling, the domestic returns with a new replacement bag which she fits in to the hoover. She starts to dust and hoover with Robert keeping an eye on the replaced bag and its unusual contents sitting innocently on the carpet by the door. When her back is turned he slips the hoover bag in to his suitcase and then, when she is finished, he is all innocence and consideration when she inquires where the bag has gone.

"Oh, don't worry. Whilst you were in the other room I gave the bag to one of your colleagues in the corridor who was emptying bins. Thanks for hoovering. I have an awful allergy."

The chamber maid seems to accept this story and leaves. Packing finished, Robert checks out at reception.

"Everything to your satisfaction, sir? Room service alright?" the young aussie girl inquires.

The girl, who cannot have been more than twenty or so had a bland, inscrutable expression. If she knew anything, she wasn't giving anything away. His secrets were safe.

"Stay was fine, thank you." Robert replies with a similar bland face.

'Lovely room and prompt service' Robert then wrote anonymously in the leather bound visitor's book. *'Will think about coming again.'*

He steps out of the foyer area and walks around to the back of the hotel. Ensuring nobody is watching, he furtively unclicks the brief case and takes out the hoover bag, placing it in the corner of the skip, just hidden under a plank of wood. Catching the bus to the airport he makes the all important call to his contact in Edinburgh. He's pulled it off yet again. *McLair-Turner's finest yet* he thinks, settling himself down on a seat. And the old boys at his grammar didn't think he'd amount to much. Well, who was the winner now? Up in the air, Robert recalls how his posh sounding surname, an uncomfortable compromise for a hybrid ex-pat like himself; was such a source of amusement to some at school. He'd never forgotten that. Bullying and homophobia was rife. Sipping hot aeroplane coffee, Robert thinks Edinburgh looks beautiful and timeless from the plane. Yet he'd outgrown the place. Yes, it had been about the need to escape and forge a new socially mobile identity, away from shameful working class Gorgie. But above all it had been about the over whelming desire to forget his former maths tutor, who would remain forever nameless - as having a name, was simply too good for him. For it was the former maths tutor who taught Robert and who used clever arguments about the beauty of abstraction to then distract his young victim to the horrific realities of homosexual rape. And Robert knows he too is now branded, and is now framed forever as both predator and victim in this intense global human jungle. Consume and hunt and be hunted and consumed – another savage irony in a world fearful and intolerant of wildness, ambiguity, shit, loss and chaos. Edinburgh slowly begins to disappear from the small aeroplane window.

The Loneliness of the Golf Sale Sign Man

Alan Crossan

Today was one of the good days. July sunlight glinted on dormant tram lines by the corner of Princes Street and Hanover Street. From here, the golf sale sign man had an uninterrupted view to the Castle perched on its volcanic rock, with temporary seating for the Tattoo being constructed on the esplanade. His eyes traced the flow of the Royal Mile past the Camera Obscura, The Scotsman building at the top of North Bridge and on to Salisbury crags and Arthur's Seat. He wondered again how many jobs offered such compensation as a view of Edinburgh on a sunny day.

It wasn't always like this. It could be miserable when the thick chilling fog of the haar rolled in from the Forth and the Castle disappeared under a curtain of cloud. His parents asked when he was going to get a proper job. Did he have no ambition to make something of his life? Why was he still working in what was only supposed to be a summer job? But the way he saw it, he was young, he had time to decide what he wanted to do, why get trapped in a career you ended up hating?

A young boy sits cross-legged in front of Super Mario,

trying to block everything else out. His father comes home from work. The boy hears him before he sees him, the slamming of doors and cursing growing louder as he approaches the boy's room. His father rips the console plug from the wall, Mario and Yoshi shrinking to a white dot. Brewery-stink on his clothes and whisky on his breath, he wants to know why the boy isn't doing his homework, oblivious to protests. Later, the back of his legs still red and stinging, his face damp, the boy decides.

He drifts in an ocean of touchscreen-distracted office workers. Failed shop fronts vanish, cocooned in board, only to unfold with new markings and luminous signs proclaiming opening day sales. Last year's festival posters disintegrate in the rain, awaiting burial under the paper and paste of a summer's renewal. Edinburgh changes, he does not. Everyone grows old on the dole, the world ages around him but he's the same boy who first raised the sign.

He accepted there wasn't a lot to his job, standing on a street corner with a luminous green sign with GOLF SALE written in black capital letters and a large arrow below pointing to his employer's shop. But aside from the view of his city, there were other benefits. The cash in hand gave him enough for a night out with his mates at the end of the week. He lived for the weekends, though recently it seemed harder to get the lads together; everyone was settling down. He felt like the last single man in Edinburgh. It was a form of social leprosy; those in relationships were naturally drawn to other couples, the singles left out in the cold to fend for themselves, survivors becoming fewer with the passing seasons.

His job was great for people-watching and all sorts passed him by: Morningside ladies out to lunch at Jenners or tourists here for the festival. It was his favourite time of the year. The city, so quiet at other times, erupted in August with crowds and the myriad street performers touting for trade. Tourists came to him for directions to different venues around town. He felt like an unofficial tour guide, an ambassador for the city. Some asked to have their photo taken with him and his sign, as if he were an attraction on a par with the Castle or Walter Scott, ready for take-off, across the street.

“You should have seen this pair this morning Davie, beautiful they were, Norwegian I think," he told his mate over a lunchtime pint in a Rose Street pub.

" Aye?"

" Aye, backpackers, just off the train at Waverley. They

wanted directions to their hostel. A blonde yin and a brunette, they both wanted photos with us."

" Course they did Lamppost, it must be your natural charm that does it or maybe it's the size of your...sign."

" Very good."

" Anyway never mind about that, we'll sort you out with a real woman tonight. You still up for that speed dating thing?"

" I'm no sure mate. It seems a bit desperate you know?"

" Don't be daft. It'll be a laugh if nothing else."

" Aye I suppose. Meet you there at eight then?"

The speed dating took place in a basement bar on George Street. A designer cocktail effort where drinks were double the price of his usual haunts and everything was shiny black or chrome. He was out of his comfort zone and he knew it. What had he been thinking agreeing to this? The women in a place like this weren't interested in a golf sale sign guy who still lived with his parents in a Stenhouse four in a block. The women here would be young professionals with their own flats in Stockbridge or the west end. He was Primark while they were Harvey Nicks. He was about to say as much to Davie when a bell rang and they were told to take a seat. He looked around and chose a free space across from an arty looking girl with red hair peeking out underneath a woollen hat and the bluest eyes hidden behind horn rimmed glasses.

" Hi I'm Alex." he said

" Hey Alex, I'm Rachel." She spoke in a clipped Home Counties accent.

" Nice to meet you Rachel."

" You too."

Silence. What were you supposed to say at these things anyway? His mind was full of Tynecastle, Rudi Skacel and pumping the Hibees and everything and nothing.

" So what do you do Alex?"

"I'm in advertising," he said, which at least wasn't a complete lie.

" Oh cool, so are you one of those Mad Men then?"

" You could say that."

" So would I know anything you've worked on?" she asked leaning in towards him.

His imagination failed him. He rubbed his sweaty palms against his jeans.

" Eh, no I doubt it."

" Oh?"

Silence again. She drummed her fingers on the table and looked at her watch. He glanced to the next table. Davie was more successful, deep in conversation with a woman in a dark blue suit, too red lipstick, dyed black hair pulled facelift tight. He overheard snatches of what they were saying: gibberish business talk. Davie was a much better exaggerator.

He tried again. "So Rachel, Do you...."

He jumped as the bell rang. His unfinished question died on his lips as Rachel's head turned to greet her next date. He sighed and pushed his chair back from the table. The guys shuffled down to their right. The ladies stayed in the same chair. He was now sitting across from Davie's former "date" .

" Hi, I'm Alex." he said.

" Heather."

" So what is it you do Heather?"

"I work out at Gogarburn, I'm a business analyst. How about you Alex?"

"Me? I work in business, acquisitions and mergers that sort of stuff. So Gogarburn, that's the big place out near the airport right? So are you one of those earning the big bonuses then?"

"I don't think that's any of your business." She crossed her arms across her chest.

"I'm sorry. I didn't mean to offend you, just making conversation like."

“It's fine."

" It's just I'm new to this sort of thing and my big mouth runs away with itself and I didn't mean..."

" I said it was fine. Just forget it." She dismissed him with a glance at her Blackberry.

Another successful date concluded, they sat, linked by one thought, willing the bell to ring. After what seemed a lifetime he was put out of his misery and moved on to the next table.

" Imagine meeting you here" she said as he sat down. He looked over. It was one of the girls who had taken his photo earlier. The blonde.

" Hey how you doing? What are you doing here?"

" That’s a fine welcome" she laughed, "Maja and I," she gestured towards her bored friend at the next table rolling her eyes at Davie's tall tales, "saw the poster outside and thought it might be good, a chance to meet people.”

" I'm just keeping my mate company. It's not really my sort of thing usually, honest!"

She laughed and raised her eyebrows at him. "I've got something to show you."

She rustled in a small bag at her feet and reappeared with a silver digital camera in her hand.

" Check it out." She handed him the camera.

It was the picture of them from the morning. There she was, weighed down with backpack, a stuffed Tweetie Pie key ring hanging from a strap, her arms wrapped jokingly around his shoulders while he stood, a gormless grin frozen across his face. It could have been a photo of a young couple, a holiday snap, were it not for the wooden pole he held and the black arrow above his head.

" It's a good one," he said passing it back. "So how long are you in Edinburgh for?"

" We're here for the festival."

" You're a bit early; it doesn't really start for another couple of weeks."

" That's ok. We wanted to see the real Edinburgh too, before all the tourists arrived. Silly I know considering that's what we are I guess."

" Not at all. If you like I could maybe show you around. If you like."

" Yes maybe."

This was easy. He was having a real conversation without a stammer or greasy palms. He wasn't waiting to get found out.

" I just realised I never got your name. I'm Alex by the way. Alex Scott. And I am a golf sale sign man."

He reached a hand across the table.

" Hello Alex Scott," she said taking his hand in hers, "I'm Astrid Hansen. It is nice to meet you." she giggled and rubbed the back of his hand with her thumb.

The bell rang and they stood up together.

The Holyrood Haggis Hunt

Barry Bensdorp

The frosty grass crackled underfoot, vapour trailed from the two heavily breathing men. They trod carefully, but manfully on the path rising up through the roiling mist which hovered in front of the huge hillock. Several paces behind, a small boy scurried along, one hand dragging a large pack and another shielded his eyes from the pale rising sun.

"S'truth it's cold," said the taller and younger of the two men, his deep voice heavily suggestive of a man from down under. He rubbed at his bare arms, trying to induce some warmth. He was now regretting his decision to come out in a black AC/DC t-shirt and ripped jeans. The second man, as craggy of face as the rising grey rock barely visible through the mist shrugged in his heavy fleece and replied in a light Scottish brogue, "Well laddie, it is the middle of January."

"Yeah but January back home is down at the beach, barbecues and a few tinnies around the pool, not flaming frostbite."

"Would you like a jacket Mr Carlton?"

"No, no, she'll be right and it's Dave, or plain old Davo for short. Let's just catch us one of these things and get back to the hotel. So, what did you call this hill again?"

"Arthur's Seat, it's the central focus of Holyrood Park and just beyond that large hedgerow is the Palace of Holyroodhouse. It's believed that even King David the First of Scotland hunted here, d'ye ken?" remarked the older man.

" I was wondering why we were going hunting in the middle of a public park, but I guess if it's good enough for a king, then it's good enough for me. I wouldn't have thought you'd get any wild life in the middle of a city though?"

"Aye, it's a common misconception. There's fish and game to be had in these locales. It's not uncommon to get an invasive type of salmon and every now and then you might spot an old trout, but that's not why we're out here at the break of dawn. This is the Holyrood Haggis Hunt, only one of its kind."

The two men paused; the mist was starting to shift in the light easterly breeze and with the merest rise in temperature as the oft vacant Scottish sun made an appearance. A little way down the hill the boy was still trying to catch up and behind him could be seen a glimpse of the grandiose roof tops of majestic Edinburgh.

"Is this the best time to hunt?" asked the young man.

"Aye, dawn or dusk. You know, early bird catching the worm," the Scottish guide said, wheezing heavily as he lit up a cigarette. He motioned for Dave to wait and as the young boy, who was also carrying a heavy doubled barrelled shotgun as well as the heavy canvas backpack finally caught up.

"Thought we were hunting haggis, not worms," smirked Davo as he rubbed some feeling back into his bare arms. Little wonder he thought that the national colours of Scotland were blue and white. He was blue with the shivering and already he felt his tan fading to white.

"Well then laddie, if you're not taking a jacket perhaps you'd care for something else to warm you up?" the Scottish guide said, handing the younger man a battered pewter flask.

"Drinking and hunting, isn't that a bit dangerous Mr Ferguson?"

"Trust me, aside from warming you up; you'll need a few good swigs of the good stuff if you want to make sure of having any chance of spotting a haggis. Take young

Kenneth here; he's never had a drink and he's never seen a haggis. Isn't that right?"

"There was the one time on Calton Hill," the wee lad replied.

"That was the shade of old Russell laddie, not a haggis."

"Russell?" asked Dave.

"Aye, was the dog I had before Kenneth. I had to let him go. Do you know how high the Council charges are for a dog licence? Robbery and rubber stamped robbery, so I replaced him with Kenneth. Would you believe I actually get money from the Assembly for the boy, but they make me pay for the dog? It was a tough choice but one of them had to go."

"Yeah mate, but the dog?"

The guide shrugged, took a long sip from the flask and handed it to Dave. The younger man took a swig, "Wow, what that wouldn't kill it's gonna cure, let's hunt haggis,"

The sun was becoming more prominent and the mist was thinning. The immense scale of Arthur's Seat filled their field of vision. Dave wondered just how they were ever going to find a haggis in this extraordinary setting. Mr Ferguson beckoned him forward down a jagged path, through some rough cut grass and stone to a small rise. He motioned for silence and pointed around him. In a reverential and almost romantic tone he simply said, "Home of the haggis," and he reached down to take the canvas pack from the small boy. He rummaged through the bag and pulled out a large swede and a large potato.

"Bait," he said taking a switchblade from his sock and began cutting the root vegetables into small cubes. He handed the cubed pieces to Kenneth. "Go on boy, up the hill and spread these around."

Kenneth stuffed the vegetables into his pockets and took off at a quick run up the path. Mr Ferguson reached back into the canvas bag and pulled out a folding stool, another flask, this one covered in dirty brown leather and a Tupperware bowl full of shortbread. "Make yourself comfortable Dave, the lad will be at least a quarter of an hour before he's back." He popped the lid off the Tupperware bowl and handed over a piece of shortbread. Unscrewing the top off the flask, he took a long drink and passed it over. Dave followed suit. "Bloody hell mate, I think it's burnt me a new throat."

"Aye, it will do that the first time and probably the second and third. So you know how to use a gun?"

"Yeah, but it's strange shooting a shotgun in the middle of a city park. Look behind us, there's all those ancient stone buildings, the one that looks like a space rocket and the Greek one on the other hill and here we are, drinking whiskey and waiting to shoot the backside out of a haggis or two with a bloody big shotgun."

"Best things to hit a haggis with. The spread of pallets as they sprint through the underbrush works best. That's the one downside with the boy. A dog is a lot quicker over the hills to flush them out and if by chance you miss the haggis and hit the dog, well you can always replace the dog."

"So what's your success rate?"

"Dogs or boys?"

"No I meant with bagging a haggis."

Mr Ferguson scratched the white stubble on his chin. "Hard to put a number on it laddie," he said taking another long drink from the flask. "There was a time when it wasn't just for tourists and for the Bard. Then again there was a time when this city was a proper city, a capital of Europe, of the world," he said in a wistful manner, sweeping his arms, his gaze taking in the views around Arthurs Seat. He tossed the flask to the younger man.

"Drink up, the boy will be back and if you want any chance of seeing a haggis, you'll need more of that down the hatch."

Two big swigs later and the young man eagerly stamped his feet. The steadily rising sun in the east was quickly burning off the last remnants of the swirling mist and in the distance, high up the hill, Dave spotted some movement. He leapt to he feet, energetically gesturing up the hillside, "Ferguson, look, the ledge up to the right."

Ferguson raised his hand to his eyes and followed the gaze of the young tourist. "That's just Kenneth, it's his brown anorak that can fool you into thinking it's something else. Give him a warning shot, it might even scare out a haggis or two," he said passing the shotgun over to Dave. The young man took it and released the safety. He pulled the stock into his shoulder and carefully followed the movement of the boy through the brush as the young lad scattered the cubes of vegetable. He took aim at a stand of hawthorn and pulled the trigger. An almighty blast echoed over the hill and Ferguson let out a cry, "Come on ye timorous beasties."

Kenneth dropped to the frosty ground at the sound of the gunshot and the whizzing of pellets only feet from where he'd been standing. He reached into his jacket pocket and pulled out a large white handkerchief. He jumped to his feet and started to sprint back down the hill, waving the white cloth over his head, bounding like a young fawn. Ferguson, ruddy of cheek and stubbly of chin, took another swig from the flask and nudged Dave, "Give them another blast, the little three legged bastards."

Dave drew a bead on the bobbing white flag, steadied his stance and eased his finger onto the trigger. He was about to pull the last quarter inch when Ferguson shouted. "Hold on, there's something else moving on the hillside. It's the colour of a dirty oat cake and it's bobbing up and down. Could it be…."

Dave swung the shotgun in the direction that Ferguson was pointing but couldn't see any sign of movement, any oat coloured object. "Shoot man, shoot," yelled Ferguson. Dave pulled the trigger, pumped the shotgun and let off a second shot, pumped again and randomly shot the hillside behind the screaming Kenneth. "Get up there Davo, go on, go," screeched the old Scotsman, "there's haggis in the hillside."

The young man lowered the shotgun to hip level and scurried up the winding path, over boulders, through rough cut grass and thistle towards the descending boy. It took about three minutes before they converged. "You could have killed me, took me eye out, left me childless," Kenneth shouted accusingly at Dave.

"Hang on, we thought there was a haggis," panted Dave, recovering his breath after the uphill slog.

"You don't really believe the old numpty, do you?"

"Jeez, I wouldn't be out on a winter's morning in a t-shirt just for a lark. Anyway's Ferguson saw something behind you, just over that ledge. Come on, let's have a look."

He hiked up the side of the imposing hill to the ledge with Kenneth following on. In the clear crisp air, he could just catch the bellows of the old Scot down below. As he crested the hill side he froze in place and heard Kenneth just behind him let out a gasp. On a flat basalt ledge, rested a three legged, oat coloured fleeced beastie. Its large brown baleful eyes stared straight at Dave and the young boy. Dave stood stock still, the heavy weight of the shotgun rested in his hands. He felt the shivering of the boy beside him. Several heartbeats past and the tableau was suddenly broken as the haggis pushed itself up to its full eighteen inches, "Not a single mention of poetry or one word of grace. Nary a single remark about pudding or I'll plant an Edinburgh kiss in your face."

Absolute Privacy

Joel M Houke

Standing on the Royal mile where it crosses North Bridge
I look west toward the castle
And think about a girl

Who, 100 years earlier
Is standing on the other side of the street
Thinking about me 100 years hence

We stand there
Separated by 12 meters and 100 years
Timidly we begin to cross the space that separates us

In the centre of the street we stop
Close enough to touch
We know we cannot

Comforted in our shared solitude
We stand together
In absolute privacy

To Be Continued...

Holyrood Books is the publishing arm of The Cooperative of Creative Writers, also known as the Writer's Cooperative.

We are always looking for new authors to work with and new material to develop and publish.

If you have something you would like to be considered for one of our publishing projects or a completed book you would like to publish through Holyrood Books, then please contact us via our website at:-
www.holyroodbooks.co.uk

Lightning Source UK Ltd.
Milton Keynes UK
UKOW032150310513

211598UK00010B/387/P

9 781849 142946